A Crooked Kind of Perfect

LINDA URBAN

 sandpiper

Houghton Mifflin Harcourt
Boston   New York

The Library of Congress has cataloged the hardcover edition as follows:
Urban, Linda.
A crooked kind of perfect/Linda Urban.
p. cm.
Summary: Ten-year-old Zoe Elias, who longs to play the piano but must resign
herself to learning the organ, instead, finds that her musicianship has a positive
impact on her workaholic mother, her jittery father, and her school social life.
[1. Organ (Musical instrument)—Fiction. 2. Music—Instruction and study—
Fiction. 3. Family life—Fiction. 4. Interpersonal relations—Fiction.
5. Schools—Fiction. 6. Humorous stories.] I. Title.
PZ7.U637Cr 2007
[Fic]—dc22 2006100622
HC ISBN: 978-0-15-206007-7
PA ISBN: 978-0-15-206608-6
Text set in Fournier
Designed by Lydia D'moch

Printed in the United States of America
DOC 10
4500530051

For my dad, Louis Urban

A Crooked Kind of Perfect

How It Was Supposed to Be

I was supposed to play the piano.

The piano is a beautiful instrument.

Elegant.

Dignified.

People wear ball gowns and tuxedos to hear the piano.

With the piano, you could play Carnegie Hall. You could wear a tiara. You could come out on stage wearing gloves up to your elbows. You could pull them off, one finger at a time.

Everybody is quiet when you are about to play the piano. They don't even breathe. They wait for the first notes.

They wait.

They wait.

And then you lift your hands high above your head and slam them down on the keys and the first notes come crashing out and your fingers fly up and down and your foot—in its tiny slipper with rubies at the toe—your foot peeks out from under your gown to press lightly on the pedals.

A piano is glamorous. Sophisticated. Worldly.

It is a wonderful thing to play the piano.

How It Is

I play the organ.
A wood-grained, vinyl-seated, wheeze-bag organ.
The Perfectone D-60.

Vladimir Horowitz

The best pianist who ever lived was Vladimir Horowitz.

Well, maybe Mozart or Beethoven or one of those ancient guys was really the best, but nobody knows because they didn't have CDs or television or anything back then. But once TV and recordings came around, the best guy for sure was Vladimir Horowitz.

I saw a show about Vladimir Horowitz one time.

I wanted to watch that old show on TV Land about the twins who are always switching names and clothes and playing tricks on their teachers and boyfriends, but my mom said, "Zoe, either you can watch PBS with me or you can go to bed." And she had popcorn.

Vladimir Horowitz was born in Russia. His mom played piano. The show didn't say what his dad did.

He was a prodigy, which means that even when he was a little kid he could play like a grown-up. When he was seventeen, he gave his first professional concert, and when he came to America a few years later, he played Carnegie Hall.

I'm ten. Almost eleven.

That means I have six years to get good.

I told my mom that I wanted to be a prodigy, that I wanted to play Carnegie Hall. I told her I wanted to play the piano.

"Take it up with Domestic Affairs," she said. That's my mom's way of saying, "Talk to your dad."

The Controller

My mom is a controller for the state of Michigan. She looks after all the money and makes sure she knows how every dime is spent and that nobody is cheating or stealing or buying stuff they're not supposed to. I found all this out on Career Day last October. I didn't know before.

On Career Day, the other moms and dads were things that kids had heard of. Like Mr. Nunzio, who is a baker and who brought us all little chocolate cupcakes with *Nunzio's Buns* written in pink frosting. Or Joella's mom, Mrs. Tinstella, who is a host of a radio program on WPOP. She had her microphone and pretended she was doing her program while she was talking to us—putting in commercials and introducing songs and taking requests—and then she gave us red-and-purple WPOP bumper stickers. For weeks afterward all the cool kids' parents had WPOP bumper stickers on their cars, but we didn't because my mom says bumper stickers fade and peel and then your car has a big gummy rectangle that attracts dirt and anyway it's just a big advertisement for WPOP and they're going to have to pay us if they want us to advertise for their noisy excuse for a radio station.

When Mrs. Trimble introduced my mom and Mom started talking about being a controller and fiscal responsibility and keeping your ducks in a row, most of the kids looked really bored. Even Mrs. Trimble looked like she was going to need to head to the teachers' lounge, which is where she goes when she has had it and desperately needs a cup of coffee and a Tylenol.

But then my mom started walking down each row and asking each kid's name, and she'd say, "Lily. Nice to meet you, Lily. Here is a quarter. Buckley. Interesting name, Buckley. Here is a nickel." She talked to each kid and gave them money and then went back up to the podium and kept on talking about how a controller has to know where every penny is and not get distracted by emotion or politics or home life or what's on the radio. Which made Joella Tinstella turn around in her seat and stare all mean at me for about five minutes. Everyone else was watching Mom. Hoping she was going to hand out more money, probably.

"In any organization there are distractions. Personalities. Drama. It is a controller's job to ignore these distractions and focus exclusively on the money," said my mom.

Then, with her eyes closed so we wouldn't think she was cheating, my mom said, "Lily, quarter. Buckley, nickel. Colton, quarter. Ashley, dime." She named every single kid in the class and said exactly which coin she gave them. "I got them all right, yes?" asked Mom and we all said yes and clapped. Mrs. Trimble said, "Thank you very much," and started telling my mom how much we all enjoyed her talk. My mom interrupted her.

"Before I go," Mom started. And my stomach started aching and my hands started sweating and I knew that every kid in my class was about to hate me.

"Before I go," she repeated, "I'll need you to pass those coins up to the front of your rows. Every penny counts. That is fiscal responsibility!" Mrs. Trimble made us all pass our coins up and Mom counted them at the end of each row, and when one quarter was missing in row three she said, "Wheeler. My quarter." Wheeler Diggs pretended that he had already passed it up to the front and then faked like Sally Marvin dropped it on the floor and he had to crawl around under his desk before he handed it over.

Later, after music class, Wheeler Diggs stopped me in the hall and looked all mean at me and I thought he was going to punch me in the stomach and I threw up and I missed my bus and my mom had to come back to school and take me home.

On Paper

The first time I told my dad that I was supposed to play the piano, he harrumphed. The second time, he rubbed his chin. The third time, he said, "That's a big commitment for a little person." My dad knows about big commitments. He has twenty-six framed diplomas from Living Room University.

"I am destined to play Carnegie Hall," I told him.

"Baby steps," he said, pulling a flyer from the stack of junk mail on the counter. It was from the Eastside Senior Center, and in it was an ad for More with Les, a revolutionary method for learning the piano. Six weeks of lessons with Lester Rennet, Award-Winning Music Teacher and Trained Motivational Speaker! Specializing in Children and Seniors! No Instrument Required!

The senior center had one piano, and it was not grand. It was an almost-upright. It leaned to one side. I guessed it had been donated by a school because there were initials carved into its legs, and if you lifted the yellow scarf off the top, you could read all about a Mrs. Pushkin who smelled like fish. The bench was bowed from years of supporting senior citizen backsides.

The More with Les students sat at folding tables. There were nine of us. Me and eight seniors, including Mr. Faber, who was ninety-two years old and slept through most of our lessons. He was not motivated by the More with Les philosophy.

"My philosophy is simple! My method revolutionary!" said Lester Rennet.

"Save it for the brochures," grumbled Mr. Faber.

"This is your More with Les songbook." The cover featured an out-of-focus photo of Lester Rennet surrounded by kids who appeared to be holding up homemade accordions. SIMPLE! it said. REVOLUTIONARY!

Mr. Rennet told us to turn to the back of the More with Les songbook. There we would find the revolution.

What I found was a piece of perforated cardboard folded over on itself a couple of times. There was a piano key design printed along the bottom edge.

"Voilà!" said Mr. Rennet.

Voilà?

"The More with Les paper keyboard!"

Paper keyboard.

The blurry kids on the songbook weren't holding accordions at all.

Lester Rennet pulled his own paper keyboard from

his briefcase and unfolded it. "As you can see," he said, holding it up to the tired piano at the front of the room, "your More with Les paper keyboard is exactly to scale. It has black keys and white keys, just like a real piano—except, of course, that they make no sound when you touch them! The More with Les paper keyboard is the perfect practice instrument! No worrying about plunking out wrong notes in front of your friends! You can practice anywhere. At the kitchen table! At Bingo Night!" Mr. Rennet pointed at me. "You can practice in the school lunchroom!"

Had Lester Rennet ever seen a school lunchroom? Did he understand that the lunchroom is a jungle, where sixth-grade beasts stalk the weak and the dorky? Unfolding a revolutionary paper keyboard would be like picking a scab in a pool of sharks—the scent of blood would cause a frenzy.

Lester Rennet continued. "Each week you will be assigned a piece from the songbook. I will play it for you here *à la piano* while you play along on your More with Les keyboard!" Then we'd go home and practice—the More with Les recommendation was twenty minutes a day—and at the following week's class we would each take a turn in "performance" at the real piano, hearing for the first time the songs our fingers had trained for all week.

"And now," said Lester Rennet dramatically, flipping my More with Les songbook to its paper keyboard page, "let us begin!" And with that he tore out the magical paper keyboard that was supposed to be my ticket to Carnegie Hall. For the first and only time, the paper keyboard made a sound: *rrrrrrrrrrrrrrrrrrrrrrrrrrrrrrrrrrrrrip*.

432

We have 432 rolls of toilet paper in our basement. Four hundred and thirty-two. This is enough to last until I'm out of high school, my mom says, provided we are conservative in our usage. She figured it out. Family of three—one of us gone almost all day every day at her office and one of us at Eastside Elementary five days a week—goes through about one roll of toilet paper a week. That means we will use fifty-two rolls in a year. 52 x 8 (the number of years until I go to college, as long as I don't flunk a grade—not likely— or skip a grade—even less likely) = 416. That leaves sixteen extra rolls for emergencies.

We have 432 rolls of toilet paper because my dad went shopping by himself. Dad is not supposed to go shopping by himself, but sometimes he gets all worked up about how he *should* be able to go shopping like everybody else. And then he gets to the store and there are lots of people around and if it is noisy or there are flashing lights—like maybe a blue flashing light announcing an extraspecial, limited-time offer on toilet paper—my dad gets really jittery, and if somebody notices and tells him something like "This is a once-in-alifetime deal that will not last," my dad will say, "I'll take it," and the people with the blue light will be very happy to help him. If he says he is going to take all of it, they will even offer to deliver it to the house. And all Dad's jitters will fade and he will believe that he has done a very smart thing, making sure that his family has enough toilet paper to last for eight years.

And then he will forget all about it.

Until the delivery truck comes to the house.

The Perfectone D-60

My dad was supposed to buy me a piano.

But instead of going online or calling Rewind Used Music, he went to the mall and it was crowded and noisy and he was walking by the big fountain with the stone hippo in the middle and he heard this sound.

This *boompa-chucka, boompa-chucka* sound.

And his toes started tapping and his hips started wiggling. The man at the store that sells Perfectone D-60s saw my dancing dad and waved him over.

Dad told me everything that happened after that. But he didn't need to. I could have figured it out for myself.

"You look like a man who knows fine music," Mr. Perfectone said to my dad. *Boompa-chucka, boompa-chucka.* "Do you play?"

My dad laughed. He was supposed to say, "My daughter is about to have a concert at Carnegie Hall. I just need to buy her a piano so she can start her lessons." But Dad was mesmerized by the *boompa-chucka-boomp.*

"Go ahead," said Mr. Perfectone, slithering around

behind my *boompa-chucka* dad. "Press a key." *Chucka-boomp.*

Dad pressed a key. A Cuban nightclub act sprang out. That's what my dad said. A single key and he could hear bongos and trumpets and guitars.

Mr. Perfectone flipped a switch. "Again," he whispered in my dad's ear. Dad was bold. He touched two keys. An entire orchestra tumbled out of the speakers. "Not bad, Mozart," Mr. Perfectone said, sliding a sales slip and a pen from his sleeve.

Two weeks later, instead of an elegant piano slick as black ice, two hairy guys dropped off a wood-grained behemoth.

Now, the Perfectone D-60 is mine.

!!!!!

The Perfectone D-60 comes with a helpful brochure. It says so right on the cover: *This helpful brochure explains the exciting features of YOUR Perfectone D-60!*

On the inside of the brochure the Perfectone D-60 people list all the exciting features which, even though they use lots of exclamation points, really aren't all that exciting.

- *Two (2!) keyboards, ergonomically stacked to put high and low octaves in easy reach!*
- *Twenty-four (24!) rhythm styles, from polka to samba to march, and eleven (11!) tempos. Or choose metronome!*
- *Ultra-Gold speaker covers, now in fashion weaves!*
- *Luxuriously realistic walnut veneer!*
- *Thirty-six (36!) orchestralike sounds (flute, oboe, marimba, violin, tuba, bassoon, piano, and more!)*

I turn on the Perfectone D-60 and flip the switch for piano. I press a key. I press two keys.

I am not excited.
I am the opposite of excited.
Never trust an exclamation point.

Maestro

My piano teacher was supposed to be a sweet, rumpled old man. I would call him Maestro and he would call me his perfect, precious star. My parents would bring me to his elegant home and he would serve us tea and I would play for him.

"A prodigy," he would say. He would discourage me from practicing too much and spoiling the spontaneity of my play.

He would take us all to parties and introduce me as the next Horowitz. I would nod to my admirers, who would not shake my hand for fear of injuring my gifted fingers.

Soon, Maestro would come to think of me as the granddaughter he never had. He would get Mom to buy me a fancy gown to wear at my concerts and have somebody do my hair so it would look all shiny and thick instead of flat, boring mud-pie brown. And then one night, just as I am about to walk onstage, he would hand me a velvet box and in it would be a diamond tiara and I would put it on and he would weep for joy.

Mabelline Person

The Perfectone D-60 comes with six months of free lessons from Mabelline Person.

The first thing you learn about Mabelline Person is that you don't say "Mabelline Person," like it is spelled, you say "Mabelline Per-*saaahn*." And the second thing is that she likes ginger ale and she expects that you will have one—preferably Vernors, in a glass, with ice—waiting for her when she arrives at your house. And the third thing is that you are never, ever, ever, supposed to set that glass of ginger ale on the Perfectone D-60.

"A-iiiiiiiiiiiiiii!" screeches Mabelline Person, grabbing the ginger ale from my hands before I can set it on the Perfectone D-60's luxuriously realistic walnut veneer. "You must have more respect for your instrument. Or your instrument will have no respect for you," she says.

Then you have to drag a big heavy armchair from across the room so that she can sit in it and watch your fingering on the keys and keep track of the notes in your music book and sigh. Not a satisfied, what-a-prodigy sigh. A what-have-I-gotten-myself-into sigh.

I know this sigh. It is the one my mother makes every time Hugh the UPS man shows up at our door with a new Living Room University package for my dad.

Mabelline Person pulls a yellow sheet of paper from her purse. It has been folded a few times and curls up at the edges. She tries to smooth it out on her lap with one hand while digging through her purse with the other. Finally, she finds a fat purple pen.

Zoe Elias, she writes. *Age 10*.

"Eleven in May," I say.

"It's January," she says. "You've had lessons before?"

I start to tell her about More with Les and the More with Les philosophy, but she holds up a many-ringed hand. "That's a yes," she says. "And for how long?"

"The More with Les method requires three clusters of lessons—each spanning a six-week period. When properly practiced, the More with Les method can produce a proficient player in a matter of—

"For how long?" she asks again.

"Four weeks," I say. "My dad . . ." I want to explain that I am not a quitter. That it is not my fault that I did not get to the More part of More with Les. My dad couldn't take it. He quit me from class. On Mondays, he'd start worrying about driving me to the Eastside

Senior Center on Thursday. He'd check every weather forecast, monitor the Eastside website for road construction information, peek in his wallet over and over to make sure his Auto Club card was in its spot. "What if there are no parking places?" he'd ask me. "What if we're halfway there and a storm sets in? What if the building is closed for repairs?"

Mabelline Person does not care to hear about my dad. She does not seem to care if I am a quitter. "Play your last lesson, please," she says.

I have to go upstairs to my room to get the More with Les songbook. When I return, Mabelline Person is reading a romance novel with half the cover torn off.

I loosen up my fingers, giving each one a pull and a wiggle, and then unfold my keyboard while Miss Person tucks her novel into her purse. "'Monkey Waltz' by Lester Rennet," I say. And then I begin. I give it my all, eager to impress upon Mabelline Person that I am a gifted musician. Even if I am only playing "Monkey Waltz," I know my innate talent will shine, showing her that I, unlike the other dull and uninspired children she is forced to teach, am a star, a chosen one, a perfect prodigy worthy of a shiny black baby grand piano.

"Great mother of Mozart," says Mabelline Person. "That was really something." She is wiping a tear from her eye—apparently, "Monkey Waltz" has touched her deeply. "Perhaps you could try again—on an instrument that produces sound?"

I fold up my paper keyboard and turn on the Perfectone D-60, which heaves a sigh just like the one Mabelline Person makes. As my fingers trip and tangle through "Monkey Waltz" I see Mabelline Person scribbling away with her purple pen. She is not writing *prodigy.*

Float Like a Butterfly

My dad is learning to be a boxing coach. He is taking another course from Living Room University, where you can learn any trade without leaving the comfort and privacy of your own home.

Already my dad has learned to Make Friends and Profit While Scrapbooking, Earn Bucks Driving Trucks, and Party Smarty: Turn Social Events into Cash Money. My dad has passed every class—even Scuba-Dooba-Do, which required him to stay underwater for a half an hour. He took the test in our bathtub breathing through a bendy straw. I timed him.

Right now, Dad is taking Golden Gloves: Make a Mint Coaching Boxing. He is on Lesson Five: Encouraging Words. He is practicing on me, even though I don't want to be a boxer. He says that the beauty of Golden Gloves is that most of the lessons are as applicable to the boardroom as they are to the boxing ring. Except for the ones about punching people.

I tell Dad I don't know what a boardroom is, but he says that doesn't matter, either. He says he can practice coaching me in anything. Which is why he is rubbing my shoulders and saying "Float like a butterfly!" while I play "Monkey Waltz" on the Perfectone D-60.

At first, this is distracting. Then it is annoying. I tell my dad to cut it out and he says, "That's right. Get mad. Get tough. Fight through the pain."

The only pain in the room is my dad.

I try to focus on the music, which is supposed to sound like dancing monkeys gracefully gliding around a sparkling monkey ballroom. Really, though, it sounds more like regular old monkeys jumping up and down on the keys.

It wouldn't sound this way on a piano, I bet. On a piano, every note would be delicate and lovely.

But I don't play the piano.

"Sting like a bee!" yells Dad.

I flip the power switch off and the Perfectone D-60 lets out an enormous sigh. "I'm taking a break."

"S'okay, champ," says Dad, rubbing my shoulders again. "You'll get 'em in round two."

Telling Emma Dent

My best friend at school is Emma Dent. I say she's my best friend at school because we don't see each other outside of school. Emma Dent lives in East Eastside. She says that all the houses there are ginormous and have great rooms and cathedral ceilings and either beige carpet or floors that look like marble. Emma Dent has three sisters and they each have their own bedroom, plus her parents have a master suite with a bathtub so big that all four Dent sisters could take a bath in it at the same time, which they would never do because that would be unsanitary.

I live in plain old Eastside, in a two-bedroom ranch house with regular ceilings. I take showers mostly.

Emma Dent says I can't come over to her house after school because her parents aren't home. Just Rosa is there, and she has enough to do watching all four Dent sisters and making sure that nobody stains up the beige carpeting and the marble-looking tile.

I tell Emma Dent that it is okay with me. And it is okay. Because even if I got invited over to Emma Dent's house in East Eastside, I probably wouldn't be able to go, because my dad would have to take me and he always gets lost and sometimes we just keep driving around and around, looking for landmarks, which there aren't any of in East Eastside, because the houses all look the same, and so sometimes we have to pull over so Dad can breathe for a while. And sometimes he has to get out his phone and call the Auto Club. Then the Auto Club calls Marty's Eastside Wreck and Tow and Marty calls Dad and tells him how to get home. Marty's a whiz at getting us back home. He says it's fun, like doing a crossword puzzle.

Anyway, all school year I've been telling Emma Dent that my parents are going to buy me a piano. I've been telling her how I am going to get private lessons and how I am going to be a prodigy and that I am going to play Carnegie Hall.

"Who is Carnegie Hall?" Emma asked.

"Carnegie Hall is not a person. It is a place," I told her. "In New York City. It's the most glamorous, most important, most famous concert hall in the world."

"My mom met Monty Hall once. In Lansing." I don't know who Monty Hall is, but Emma said his name like I was supposed to. Kind of like she said Lansing, like it was as glamorous and important and famous as New York City. Which it is not.

Today, our first day back from Christmas break, I was going to tell Emma about the Perfectone D-60. How my dad had cast my dreams upon a rocky shore. How my genius might never blossom. How my life as a prodigy was over.

I was going to tell her about ball gowns that would never be worn, ovations that would never be heard, fan mail that would never be read.

I was going to bare my soul to my dear best friend Emma Dent and, through tragedy, we would forge an unbreakable sisterly bond.

But Emma is not sitting at our regular lunch table. She is two tables away, sharing a bag of SnackyDoodles with Joella Tinstella.

"Me and Joella are best friends now," Emma says. "We hung out all Christmas vacation. She lives right in East Eastside, just a block away. You can sit with us until you find a new best friend if you want."

If I had my paper keyboard, I could unfold it now and start practicing. It really wouldn't make any difference.

I have gone over to the dork side.

Here's the Story

Most of the time after school, I do Dad's Living Room University lessons with him. Last week we finished Golden Gloves. Now we're doing Roger, Wilco, Over, and Cash! Learn to Fly Like the Pros. We're up to Lesson Four: Take Off!

"Okay, Dad." I read from the instruction manual. "Press the ignition button."

Dad stares at the table. He is holding a frying pan lid in his left hand and waving his right hand over the household items we have set up according to the Roger, Wilco mock cockpit instructions. "The saltshaker, Dad. Press the saltshaker."

I reach over to point it out, knocking over the Cheez Whiz and a couple of containers of dried herbs.

"Maybe I need to fly solo for a while, honey." Dad puts the oregano back on the altimeter spot. "Why don't you practice your organ lesson?"

The Perfectone D-60 looks a little bit like the real cockpit photo in the Roger, Wilco manual. There are lots of buttons and switches and flashing lights that go on and off depending on which of the twenty-four rhythm styles you choose. Miss Person says I'm not supposed to be playing with the rhythm styles yet. She says that for three whole months I'm not to use anything but metronome, which just goes *tock tock tock* and is boring, and so even though I've only been playing for one month and one week, I keep testing out my lessons with different rhythm styles so I don't fall asleep at the keyboard.

Which I wouldn't have to do if I was practicing the piano.

Practicing the piano is never boring.

There are whole movies about people practicing the piano.

I saw one movie about this curly-haired kid who heard a piano recital on the radio and the next day her parents got her lessons and a real piano. And a teacher came and told her to play scales, which she hated. Everybody in piano movies has to play scales. They all say they hate playing scales, but they do it anyway and then the movie shows you lots of close-ups of hands playing scales. The hands start out small like that curly-haired girl's and then they change into teenager hands and then grown-up hands and then the next time you see her she's not a kid, she's a grown-up in a ball gown playing Beethoven at Carnegie Hall.

When you play the organ, you don't play scales.

And you don't play Beethoven, either. Mostly, you play old television theme songs from the Perfectone D-60 lesson book.

Already I can play "The Ballad of Gilligan's Isle" and "The *Scooby-Doo* Theme." This week's lesson is *The Brady Bunch* song. It's kind of easy. I play it a bunch of times with the Perfectone D-60's Metronome switch on, and then I flip a switch labeled Western Swing.

"That's pretty good, honey," says Dad.

"It sounds okay," I say. *For an organ,* I think. "Want to hear it on Cha-Cha?"

"Lay it on me," says Dad.

I press a button and a peppy beat kicks in. Until we got the Perfectone D-60, I had never heard a cha-cha. It's like two shoes dropping on the floor and then a dog scratching himself. *Whump whump cha-cha-cha, whump whump cha-cha-cha.* Like that.

Dad is dancing around the living room. I push Steel Drum and Marimba on the Perfectone D-60.

"Olé!" says Dad. Then he starts singing—*cha-cha-cha*—about a lovely lady—*cha-cha-cha*.

By the time he gets to the "three boys of his own" part, I have flipped the rhythm switch to Polka and the keyboard is pumping out accordion sounds. Dad keeps singing, but now he's bouncing and spinning around the room and using some kind of accent, saying "vun day" and "dis vellow."

He does a hoppy kind of twirl. "Dis is a vonderful polka, Zoe," he says. "Just vonderful."

"Thank you," I say.

"But I am getting voozy from de spinning."

I flip a couple of switches, swapping Tuba for Accordion and changing the rhythm to March.

Dad grins and dashes out of the living room to grab two pot lids he's been using for his DC-10 course. He marches back and forth across the carpet with his knees high in the air, singing and crashing his cymbals together after every "bunch." *Crash-crash!*

"Big finish!" I yell, and Dad tosses a pot lid up in the air, spinning to catch it behind his back. He misses. The lid rolls into the hallway and clatters on the linoleum.

I peek around the Perfectone D-60 to see where it has landed. It's at Mom's feet. She's home from work. With all our playing and singing, we didn't hear her come in.

"Let me guess, Living Room University has added a drum major course?" she says. She tosses Dad his runaway cymbal. "Where's dinner? I'm starving."

"Couldn't cook," says Dad. "All the measuring cups are in the mock cockpit."

Mom sighs.

"Wing Ping Linguini?" asks Dad. That's his favorite BBQ-Chinese-Italian restaurant. The food isn't good, but they deliver.

"Not in the budget. We're still crawling out of the financial hole created by this marching band of yours." Mom tilts her head toward the Perfectone D-60.

Dad sits. His pot lids clang together in his lap.

"It's okay, honey," says Mom. "We'll have frozen pizza."

Dad nods and heads to the kitchen.

Mom turns to me. "Shouldn't you be playing scales or something?"

You Are Invited

Right before Valentine's Day a pink envelope comes in the mail, which I think maybe could be a valentine from a secret admirer or something but it is not. It is an invitation: pink, in the shape of a sneaker, with a big silver bow where the laces should be.

We're having a Birthday Party!
And this invitation's for you!
We want you to come and have lots of cool fun!
It will sure be a Really Big Shoe!

WHO: *Emma Dent*
WHAT: *An 11th Birthday Party—*
Bring Your Dancing Shoes!!
WHERE: *31 Superior Drive, East Eastside*
WHEN: *Saturday, March 6, 4 P.M.*
WHY: *Because You Are One of Emma's Best Pals!!!*

Emma Dent has invited me to her birthday party. Me. Her former best friend. But the invitation says I am one of her best friends. Am. Like, right now. Actually, it says "best pals," but that's really the same thing.

Maybe she and Joella had a fight. Maybe Emma was always talking about me and how much fun we used to have at lunch talking about whatever it was we used to talk about. And then maybe Joella got jealous and told Emma that if she liked me so much why didn't she just marry me, which is all babyish and stupid, but exactly the kind of thing that a stupid babyish person like Joella would say. And then Emma said, "Fine!" and Joella said, "Fine!" And then maybe Emma felt all rotten about how she treated me and she didn't know what to say. So she invited me to her birthday party and prayed that I would come and forgive her. Which, of course, I will.

I look at the invitation again and see something written behind the silver shoelace bow.

Shhhhhhhhhhhhhhhhh! Don't tell Emma!
This is a surprise party!

Emma Dent did not invite me to her Really Big Shoe birthday party.

Her mother did.

For the Girl Who Has Everything

I tell my dad that I need dancing shoes for Emma Dent's birthday party.

And he tells my mom.

And she says that my regular shoes will be fine and what kind of parent throws a party where kids have to go out and buy special shoes, isn't it enough that we have to spend twenty dollars on a birthday present?

We don't spend twenty dollars, though. We spend $14.98. Plus shipping.

"What kind of birthday present do you bring to a Really Big Shoe party?" I ask Dad.

"Odor-Eaters?"

"Dad!"

"How about socks?"

Socks might be okay. The first time me and Emma talked was in third-grade square dancing. We were changing into our gym shoes and Emma noticed we were both wearing toe socks. And when we had to pick partners, she picked me and that was it. Best friends.

"Socks sound good," I say.

Me and Dad spend the whole afternoon shopping

online for socks. We order a bunch from this website called *Sock-It-to-Me*. We get pink ones with sparkly pigs, and some turquoise ones with crocodiles in sunglasses, and two pairs of stripy toe socks: one for me and one for Emma. Like old times.

Emma Dent's Really Big Shoe

Emma Dent's party is on a Saturday afternoon, which means that even though my mom goes in to work most Saturdays, she can come home in time to drive me to Emma's. Which is good, because Eastside Wreck and Tow closes early on Saturdays and if Dad got lost we might have to sit in the car until Monday when Marty opens up so we could call him and he could tell us how to get back home.

I've got my feet up on the dashboard. I stare at my regular shoes, which are not made for dancing.

"New socks," says Mom.

I can't tell if she says it like it's a good thing, like "Cool, new socks!" or if it's a bad thing, like "Where did you get the money for new socks?"

I like these socks. They have all my favorite colors striping through them. Turquoise. Sea green. Teal. Navy. Turquoise. Sea green. Teal. Navy. You can't tell with my regular shoes on, but the toes are pink.

Maybe I'll take my shoes off to dance.

"Thirty-one Superior Drive, right? Is this the house?" asks Mom.

There is a huge, inflatable, high-heeled shoe hovering above the patches of snow in the front yard.

"I think so."

"I'll be back at six, Zoe. Can you be ready, so I don't have to get out of the car?"

"Okay," I say.

"If you need me, call the office," Mom says.

I grab Emma's present and dash up the walk.

Mrs. Dent opens the door for me. "It's Zoe Elias!" she yells.

"Aaawwwwwwwwwwww."

"We thought you might be Emma," says Mrs. Dent. "The other girls are in the media room."

The media room has a huge flat-screen television and a wall full of DVDs and posters for movies I've never heard of and marble-looking tile. It also has ten fifth graders smooshed together on an L-shaped couch.

"Hi," I say.

"Hi," they say, all at the same time.

None of them move. There is no more room on the couch. I stand next to a poster for something called *Death Wish II*.

"You can put your present over there," says Joella

Tinstella, pointing to a TV tray with lots of little pink presents stacked on it.

I put my present where she tells me to. Then I return to my *Death Wish* spot.

Joella is wearing silver clogs with colored rhinestones that spell out BRAT. Britt Munsch is wearing them, too, only hers are shiny red and the BRAT part is gold. Everyone is wearing those Brat shoes. Except for Lily Parker. Lily Parker is wearing sandals with heels that must be three inches high. She sees me staring at them.

"They're my sister's. She's an eighth grader. She got them for the Winter Wonderland Dance at East Eastside Middle School. She went with Danny Parker. No relation."

No relation. Still, it would be kind of weird going out with a boy with your own last name. Actually, it would be kind of weird going out with a boy at all.

"Girls! This is it!" Mrs. Dent shushes us and everybody who has been sitting on the couch runs to hide behind it. I squat behind the present table.

"Mom," we hear Emma say, "there's, like, a big shoe in the yard."

"SURPRISE!" we yell. And then everybody who

was behind the couch pops out and starts laughing and hopping up and down and their clogs are clattering on the marble-looking tile. Nine—no, ten, counting Emma's—ten pairs of noisy, shiny, sparkling clogs.

And not a sock in sight.

Everybody Knows That

There is a lot of squealing when Emma opens her presents. First she gets some lip gloss, which she has to try on right away.

Joella Tinstella gasps. "You look like that girl on *The Beach*!" she says, and then everybody squeals and nods. Except me. I don't watch *The Beach*.

Emma opens some gift cards and some CDs. More squealing.

And then Lily Parker gives her a red T-shirt that says BRAT in gold and Emma likes it so much she has to run to the bathroom to take off the pink Brat shirt she is wearing and put on Lily's red Brat shirt and when she comes back into the media room and does this model pose thing, everyone squeals again.

And then she opens my present.

And she gets socks.

There is no squealing.

Emma stares at the socks. Then she shoves her hand into one of them, like she thinks that her real present must be inside. There is nothing inside except Emma's hand.

"Time for cake and dancing!" says Mrs. Dent.

Emma puts the socks down behind her CDs and gift cards and we all follow Mrs. Dent to what she says is the great room, which is really just a kitchen and a living room put together. On the kitchen island is a fancy grocery-store cake in the shape of a shoe. Emma blows out the candles and everyone cheers and somebody puts on some music and people start dancing. Mrs. Dent cuts the cake, and while she is handing out slices I hear Joella say to Britt that even Emma's mom doesn't wear socks.

"Nobody wears socks. Everybody knows that," she says.

I decide not to dance.

I sit on my feet and cover up my regular shoes and my stripy socks.

I eat shoe cake.

I wait for six o'clock.

5:45

Mrs. Dent turns off the CD player. "Girls, there is one last present. Follow me!"

We follow Mrs. Dent down the hallway and to a room with double doors.

"Voilà!" she says, flinging open the doors.

There, with a ginormous pink bow wrapped around it, is a gleaming white grand piano.

6:00

I get in the car.

"Shhhh," says Mom. "Horowitz."

She is listening to WCLS, the classical station. They're playing a recording of Beethoven's "Moonlight Sonata." I close my eyes and try to forget about Brat clogs and grand pianos.

When we pull into our driveway, I open my eyes.

Mom has closed hers. She's sitting there, letting the car run. The corners of her mouth are turned up a little. She looks happy.

I close my eyes again.

I wonder what Mom is thinking.

Maybe she is thinking about me.

Maybe she is thinking about me thinking about her.

Maybe she is wondering if I had a good time at the party and if I like parties and if maybe I would finally like to have a real birthday party when I turn eleven in May.

Or maybe she is thinking about work.

"Bravo!" shouts someone on the radio. "Bravo!" We listen to the people on the recording cheer and then

Mom takes the key out of the ignition and the applause disappears.

"Nobody wears socks anymore," I tell her.

"Not even in Michigan? In March? When there's still snow on the ground?"

"Nobody."

"You wear socks," Mom says.

"Exactly," I say.

Are You Ready to Rumba?

"That was fine," says Mabelline Person. She gulps the last of her ginger ale and stretches.

"Next week . . ." She flips the page from today's lesson, "Green Acres," to the next song in the Perfectone D-60 songbook, "Those Were the Days," which the book says is the theme from some show called *All in the Family.*

"Scootch," she says.

I move off the bench so she can sit and play the song for me. Like everything else I've learned, "Those Were the Days" is mostly melody, so Mabelline Person's right hand moves around a lot on the top keyboard, but her left hand just plays a couple of chords on the bottom keys. C. G. C. G. She yawns.

"Keep the metronome speed on four," she says.

"Okay," I say.

She looks at her watch, then folds up her yellow papers and puts them in her purse. She stretches again. She looks at her watch again.

"Any questions?" she says.

"Nope," I say.

She looks at her watch *again.*

"Okay," she says finally. "I'm off."

As soon as the door clicks behind her Dad peeks into the living room.

"She's gone?" he asks.

"She's gone," I say.

"Well, then," says Dad, holding up a silver spatula like a microphone. "ARE YOOOU READY TO RUUUUMBAAAAAAAAAAAA?"

I flip the rhythm switch to Rumba, push the tempo up to six, and start again on "Green Acres."

And then Dad starts singing, holding up the spatula like a pitchfork and hooking his thumb on the strap of his imaginary overalls.

I add a couple of trills—little flutterings of notes—to spice things up.

Dad sings about farm living. He shakes his hips.

I switch the rhythm to Tango and change my playing to fit.

Dad puts the spatula between his teeth and tangos across the room, then spits the spatula out for his finale. But before he can sing a note, the doorbell rings.

It's Mabelline Person.

"That was you playing that. I saw you through the window. That was you," she says.

"I'm sorry," I say. "I know I'm supposed to stick to metronome."

She stomps into the living room and starts flipping pages in the Perfectone songbook. Finally she stops at "I Dream of Jeannie."

"Watch," she says.

I watch. Not only does her right hand fly around the upper keyboard, but her left hand moves pretty quickly, too.

"See my foot?" she asks.

Her foot? There are pedals attached to the Perfectone D-60. Ten of them. I've stepped on them getting on and off the bench, and I know that they play different notes, but I've never had to use them in a song before.

"These letters across the top indicate what pedals you play," she says over her shoulder. She is still playing "I Dream of Jeannie." "The pedals are arranged just like keys on the keyboard. See? B-C-D-E-F-G-A-B-C-D, plus sharps and flats. I want to see what you can do with this next week."

Miss Person gets up and goes to the armchair. She pushes her hand around under the cushion. "There they are," she says, pulling out her keys.

"You?" She points at me. "Metronome."

"And you?" She whirls around to face Dad, who is hiding in the curtains. "Maybe a belly dance for this one."

Hugh

The only grown-up my dad really talks to in person, other than Mom, is Hugh the UPS guy. Hugh has big teeth and a bushy mustache. He's bald and in the winter you can see steam rise off his head.

Hugh just delivered Dad's latest Living Room University course: Rolling in Dough: Earn a Dolla' Baking Challah. He's sitting at our kitchen table having a cup of coffee.

"One time," says Hugh, "I'm dropping off a package for this old guy and he says, 'Hey, I got a thing I need shipped. You got a big box?' Now, normally, I tell people that they gotta find their own boxes, right?"

"Right," says Dad.

"But this guy is a true geezer and I got a spare box in the truck, so I give it to him, right?"

"Right."

"And he looks at the box and says it's kinda small, but if he curls the thing up, he might be able to get it in the box okay. But he's gonna need some help, 'cause the thing he's gotta ship is kinda heavy, right?"

"Right," me and Dad say together.

"So, I got a light day and this old guy seems real

confused about how he's gonna pack this heavy thing up, so I go in to help him, right?"

"Right."

"So the old guy, he leads me through the house and into his bathroom and I'm thinking this is weird, but I go with it, and he flips on the bathroom light and what do you think is in there?"

Me and Dad don't know.

"An alligator! The guy's got a three-foot alligator in his bathtub! And I'm flipping out! I jump up on the toilet so I'm out of the reach of these alligator jaws and I'm screaming like a girl—no offense, Zoe—but it's a flippin' alligator!"

Dad's eyes are wide and I'm laughing, picturing big, bald Hugh balancing on a toilet seat, screaming his head off.

"And the old guy starts yelling, 'She's dead! She's dead, you idiot! She's not gonna bite you, she's dead!'" Hugh takes a swig of coffee and shakes his head. "Turns out his bathtub alligator—Ramona was her name—died that morning and the guy wants to ship her down to Florida to his ex-wife, thinking she'll bury Ramona near a swamp or something so Ramona can feel at home during her long dirt nap."

"Did you help him?" I ask.

"I'm not touching no just-dead alligator!" says Hugh. "UPS wouldn't ship it, anyway. But I love imagining his ex-wife opening up a big old box thinking she won the sweepstakes and finding a dead alligator grinning at her."

Me and Dad laugh. Hugh's almost done with his coffee, but I don't want him to stop telling stories. "Is that the craziest customer you ever had?" I ask.

"Probably the craziest, yeah. But we get lots of them. Just yesterday I'm over in East Eastside and this lady sees my truck and comes running out of her house through the snow in her bare feet telling me she's got a return to do and what would it cost to ship a grand piano. Crazy, right?"

"Right," I say.

In the Pink

"Does anyone here know how to play an instrument?" Mrs. Trimble asks. Our regular music teacher, Mr. Popadakis, has pinkeye and isn't here today, so Mrs. Trimble has to take over.

"I play violin," says Hector Kheterpohl.

Mrs. Trimble looks around the music room. There are no violins in here, just an upright piano and a plastic box full of percussion instruments: tambourines, maracas, bells, a triangle. Mrs. Trimble passes them around the room.

"Emma has a piano," says Britt.

"Not anymore," says Emma. "I took one lesson and I hated it, so my mom sold it to Rewind Used Music and got me this awesome DJ station. I got a turntable and CD player and some amps and all this cool stuff that my dad has to figure out. Then we can have dances at my house and me and Joella can be the DJs."

"I already know how to be a DJ because of my mom," says Joella. Like we'd forget. Like Joella doesn't wear a WPOP T-shirt every day she's not wearing a Brat shirt.

"Well, we don't have a DJ station in here," says Mrs. Trimble. "I guess we'll just have to shake these things and sing something. 'Old MacDonald'?"

Sometimes I think Mrs. Trimble forgets we are in fifth grade.

"You have a piano, don't you?" Emma asks me.

"An organ," I say.

"That's close enough," says Mrs. Trimble. "Come play something and we'll all sing along. Do you know 'Old MacDonald'?"

I don't know "Old MacDonald." But I know "Green Acres." It feels different to play on one long keyboard, but I figure out where to put my hands and I start playing. At first, I miss the Perfectone D-60's Rumba switch, but pretty soon everybody is shaking their tambourines and maracas and it sounds okay.

"Are there words to this song?" asks Mrs. Trimble, and a couple of kids laugh. And then Wheeler Diggs starts singing about the land spreading out both far and wide. You can tell which kids watch TV Land because they know the words, too, and sing with him.

When "Green Acres" is over everybody claps. And then Mrs. Trimble asks if I know another one and I play "The *Scooby-Doo* Theme." Almost everybody knows the words and people are singing and laughing and I start feeling like it would be okay if Mr. Popadakis had pinkeye forever.

But then the bell rings for lunch and Mrs. Trimble makes everybody pass their instruments to the front and Emma and Joella start talking about how when they have dance parties there will be real music and we all head back to our classroom to get our lunch bags.

And Wheeler Diggs bumps me in the hall. "That was cool," he says, and he punches me in the arm, which hurts a little, but in a good way.

Wheeler Diggs

Wheeler Diggs never does his homework.

He never answers in class.

He always buys a milk shake and a plate of Tater Tots for lunch.

He calls most people by their last names: Polzdorfer, Olivetti, Mueller, Shell.

He wears orange sneakers and his jeans are ripped and raggedy at the hem. He wears a faded jean jacket all the time, even indoors, even when it is sticky hot out. And in the winter, he doesn't put another coat on over it, either. Just shoves a U.S. Army sweatshirt on underneath.

Usually, Wheeler Diggs is a mess.

Except his hair.

On anybody else, his curly hair might look goofy, but on Wheeler Diggs it looks just the right kind of wild. And it's dark, which makes his blue eyes look even brighter. And his smile, which is kind of lop-sided, looks like he's trying not to smile, but he can't help it.

Which is why, sometimes, every once in a while,

somebody will smile back. And sometimes, most of the time, those people will get punched in the stomach. Which is why even the kids who sit with him at lunch are a little bit scared of him and why, really, Wheeler Diggs doesn't have a best friend, either.

I Dream of Jeannie

"Slow the metronome down. Put it on three," says Miss Person.

I slow it down. This is my second week of playing "I Dream of Jeannie" and my feet keep tripping over the pedals. My hands, though, are doing what they're supposed to.

"Okay," she says. "That wasn't horrible. You're getting used to the pedals, and your fingering was pretty good." She scribbles something on her yellow papers.

"Am I a prodigy?" I ask.

Miss Person snorts. She pushes the cap back on her purple pen. "You have some talent and you work hard. I'll take that over prodigy any day."

Hearing that makes me feel good. But not as good as being called a prodigy would have.

"Is your dad around?" she asks.

"Dad!" I yell.

"Sweet brother of Bach, don't yell like that. You'll apoplex me."

Dad comes into the room. He's wearing a Living Room University apron and has flour up to his elbows.

"I don't usually do this with beginners," Miss Person tells him. "But I'm recommending your daughter go to the Perfectone Perform-O-Rama this year. She's ten, right? When's her birthday?"

"May fourteenth," I say before Dad can answer.

"Just our luck. The competition starts on May fifteenth. She'll have to compete against the eleven-year-olds—most of them will have been playing for a couple of years—but I don't think she'll embarrass herself."

"Where is the Perform-O-Rama?" asks Dad.

"Birch Valley," says Mabelline Person. She pulls a flyer out of her purse. "At the Birch Valley Hotel and Conference Center. May fifteenth and sixteenth."

"Is that a weekend?" asks Dad.

"Yes. There are performances Saturday and Sunday—with awards on Sunday afternoon."

I see Dad relax. The Perform-O-Rama is only an hour away and on a weekend. That means Mom can take me and Dad won't have to drive or be around all those people.

"I'll have to check our schedules, but it sounds good to me," says Dad.

"Fine, then," says Miss Person. "Let's get back to work."

Hey, I think. *How come nobody asked me if I want to do this?* And that's what I say.

Miss Person is quiet.

Dad is quiet.

"I'm sorry, honey," he says. "Do you want to play at the Perform-O-Rama?"

I think about how it felt to have my fingers gliding over those keys, how Miss Person looked when I finished playing. It felt good. Really good. Not as good as it would to play the piano, but . . .

"YES!" I yell.

"Mozart's postman!" gasps Miss Person.

I flip on the metronome and let my fingers dream of Jeannie all over again.

The Perfectone Songbook

At our next lesson, Mabelline Person gives me a CD and a stack of Perfectone songbooks: *Marvelous Movie Memories, Hits of the Fifties, Hits of the Sixties, Hits of the Seventies, Hits of the Nineties.*

"What about the eighties?" I ask.

"There were no hits in the eighties," says Miss Person.

Sticky notes with numbers scribbled on them are stuck to some of the songbook pages. "I've made a recording of each of the songs I think might work for you. You can tell which is which by the numbers on the stickies," she explains. "Listen. Look at the music. Try out a couple of the melodies. Two weeks from now, we'll need to start working exclusively on your Perform-O-Rama selection."

"Two weeks?"

"Do you not own a calendar? There are only seven weeks until the Perform-O-Rama. We really ought to pick next week, but I want you to get in one more week of pedal work before we select a piece," she says.

Only seven weeks! I think. "Chopin's toaster!"

"You said it," says Miss Person.

Another Way the Organ
Is Not Like the Piano

When you play piano, you don't go to Perform-O-Ramas. You give recitals.

A recital is a dignified affair.

There are candelabras at a recital.

People sit in velvet chairs and sip champagne and look over the program. There are always programs at a recital.

At a recital, you play Mozart and Beethoven and Strauss and Bach.

You do not play *Hits of the Seventies*.

Zsa Zsa Goober

Something is horribly wrong with the lunchroom.
Fireside Scouts have taken over.

Three tables are covered with green cloths and
pyramids of Fudgy-Buddies and Minty-Chips. Which
means there are three fewer tables for sitting at. Which
means that a sixth grader has taken my until-you-get-
a-new-best-friend spot at Emma Dent's table.

There are fourth graders at third-grader tables.
There are sixth graders at fifth-grader tables.
There are boys sitting near girls.
Anything could happen.

"Hey, Goober!" I hear Wheeler Diggs yell. He's
looking at me. I'm Goober?

"Zsa Zsa Goober! Come here!"

Now I get it. Zsa Zsa Gabor. *Green Acres.*

"Actually, it was Eva Gabor in *Green Acres,*" I tell
him. "Zsa Zsa was her older sister. I saw a thing about it
on TV Land. And it's pronounced Gah-bore, not—"

"Sit down, Goober," he says.

I sit. It is the only free seat in the room.

"Eat your lunch," he says.

I eat.

And then Wheeler Diggs and the other boys go back to all the stuff they were doing before I got to the table. Eating and pushing each other and burping. Mostly burping.

They really like burping.

"Baby burp," says Colton Shell. He lets out a tiny, high-pitched one.

"Earthquake!" says Henry Olivetti. His burp is loud and rumbly.

"Hot lava!" yells Colton. It is difficult to tell the difference between an earthquake burp and a hot lava burp, but I don't say anything.

"Outer space!" says Henry.

"You can't burp in outer space," I say.

It's true. You can't. I learned it when Dad was taking Living Room University's The Final Frontier: Put Cash in Your Pocket While Flying a Rocket, Lesson Fifteen: Out to Launch. I tell them that there's this valve thing at the top of your stomach that hangs open a little bit so burp gas can escape, but when you're in space there's no gravity and the hamburger or yogurt or whatever you were eating floats up and presses that valve closed. So no gas can get out. So you can't burp.

"Bet I could." Henry lets out another Earthquaker.

"If that's true, about the food and everything, then you couldn't burp upside down, either," says Wheeler.

"Guess not," I say.

"Bet I could," say Henry and Colton at the same time.

Sally Marvin bounces up to the table. "Anybody want to buy some Minty-Chips?"

Henry and Colton burp a "No."

Sally is disgusted, but she is in uniform and sticks it out for the Scouts. "We'll be here all month." She eyeballs Wheeler Diggs's raggedy jeans. "And we don't take credit."

I want to tell Sally to get lost, but when I open my mouth no words come out. Instead, I launch an Earthquaker that makes Henry Olivetti beam with pride.

Another Diploma

My dad is a Biscotti Hottie.

That's what it says on his diploma for Bake Your Way to the Bank: Turning Cookies into Cash.

"Congratulations," I say.

"Thank you," he says. "Now what are we going to do with all these cookies? The freezer is full from Rolling in Dough."

There are cookies everywhere.

Fat, plastic zippy bags of cookies.

Chocolate Chip. Oatmeal Raisin. Carmel Nut Clusters. Zing-Bang-Doodles. Madeleines. Coconut Igloos. Lemon Melvins. Barney Goo-Goos. Butterscotch Biscotti. Pecan Sandies. Haystacks. Molasses Chums. Marshmallow Puff-Daddies. Cornmeal Bows. Bada-Bings. Maple Macaroons. Shortbread. Gingerbread. Almond Mandelbrot. Icebox Swirly-Qs. Cinnamon Crackles. Figgy Cram-Handies. Brazen Hussies.

"Did you give any to Hugh?" I ask.

"Three bags full," says Dad. "He wouldn't take any more."

"You could put a few in my lunch," I say.

"Perfect!" says Dad.

Fireside Chat

"What's in the box, Goober?" asks Wheeler Diggs. He pushes aside his Tater Tots to make room on the lunch table.

"You'll find out when you stop calling me Goober," I say.

"Fine, Zsa Zsa. What's in the box?"

It's a big box, almost too big for me to carry. It is full of cookies.

"Beastly!" says Colton. I think this is a good thing.

"Extremely beastly," I say. "Help yourself."

He does. And Henry Olivetti does, too. And a bunch of the other boys: Danny Polzdorfer, Mario Pollack, Felix and Oscar Mellenderry. Pretty soon our lunch table is surrounded by kids.

"Help yourself," I say again.

"These are awesome!" Danny Polzdorfer is monopolizing the Maple Macaroons.

"Out of the way, Dorf," says a sixth grader. "What do you got that's chocolate?"

I point out the Swirly-Qs and the Brazen Hussies. Joella and Emma slide into the crowd.

"Puff-Daddy?" I offer.

"We're dieting," says Joella. Emma doesn't say anything. She loves marshmallows. Passing up a Puff-Daddy must be killing her.

"Where'd you get all this?" asks somebody with a Haystack.

"My dad made them."

Kids are shoving their way to the table, hollering about Molasses Chums and Zing-Bang-Doodles. Crumbs are flying. And then, suddenly, it is quiet.

A wall of Fireside Scouts has circled the table.

"What's going on here?" says Sally Marvin. "Are you trying to ruin our business?"

Beethoven's lunch lady! The Fireside Scout cookie sale!

"I forgot," I say.

"Forgot?" a red-headed scout says. Her fingers are all twitchy and she looks like she wants to tie me in a slipknot, or whatever kind of knot it is that Fireside Scouts do. "You bring buckets of cookies to school so often that you just forgot about our sale?"

It's a box, actually. A UPS box. Not a bucket at all. I suspect this is not her point.

"I really forgot. My dad had all these extra cookies . . ."

Red pokes me in the chest. "You just made enemies with the Fireside Scouts of America."

I Don't Need No Stinking Badges

When I was eight, I wanted to be a Fireside Scout.

I made one of those sashes out of paper towels and drew a bunch of badges on it and I used to wear it around the house sometimes.

But I never was a Fireside Scout.

Fireside Scout meetings are after school and they last an hour and a half, which means you can't take the bus home. So somebody who works, who might be in the middle of a meeting or something, would have to go get her coat and boots and everything on and go pick you up and drive you home and then drive all the way back across town to the office, because it's only four-thirty and work doesn't get done all by itself.

So even if I wanted to be a Fireside Scout, I couldn't.

But I don't want to be one now.

Which turns out to be a good thing.

The Wheeler on the Bus

"Zsa Zsa!" It's Wheeler Diggs. What is he doing on the bus?

"My brother used to drive me, but he joined the army," says Wheeler.

"Sorry," I say.

"You got any more cookies?"

"Not with me. There are another couple of boxes at home. I can bring you some tomorrow—as long as the Fireside Scouts don't find out."

"Can't wait that long. I'm hungry now. Where do you live?"

"Eastside," I say.

"Duh, Goober. Everybody on this bus lives in Eastside."

"Zsa Zsa," I remind him. "I live on Grouse Avenue, right by Warbler." Lots of the streets in Eastside are named after Michigan's native birds.

"Close enough," says Wheeler.

And when the bus gets to my stop, Wheeler Diggs gets off and follows me home.

Who Is This Kid?

Wheeler Diggs follows me all the way into my house.

My dad is in the kitchen, baking and listening to Miss Person's CD. He is singing along to something from *Hits of the Seventies*. "Oh my dar-lin' . . ."

"Dad, this is Wheeler Diggs," I say.

Dad stops singing. He stares at me. Then he stares at Wheeler. Then he stares at me again.

"You bake a fine cookie, sir," says Wheeler.

Sir? Wheeler Diggs said sir?

Dad still doesn't say anything.

"Especially the Lemon Melvins. Top drawer."

Top drawer? What is he talking about? Who is this kid?

Dad swallows. "Thank you," he says. "Would you like another?"

And just like that, Wheeler Diggs is sitting at our kitchen table talking cookies with my dad. Dad is explaining the difference between baking soda and baking powder and why you have to beat the eggs before you put them in cookie dough and just how important it is to preheat an oven. And Wheeler is eating it all up. The cookies. And the cookie talk.

This is what Dad and I do. We talk about his Living Room University classes. He gives me cookies. How can he share all this with some kid who just shows up at the house one day?

"It's pretty simple," Dad is saying. "Here, you want to try?"

I watch Wheeler Diggs put on an apron and crack eggs. In my house. With my dad.

"Dad," I say. "I have to make a decision about my Perform-O-Rama song."

"That's okay, Zoe. You go ahead. This young man and I won't bother you. What's your name again?"

Wheeler tells him and Dad repeats it: "Wheeler." And then Dad asks Wheeler if he'd like to take his jacket off and Wheeler says no, because he never takes his jacket off, and Dad says okay and then Wheeler and Dad start making cookies together and I take the CD player into the living room, because if I don't I'll look like a dork for making such a big deal about picking my song.

I set the CD player for the next song on my list.

Miss Person is playing the song with a samba beat.
There it is, in the *Hits of the Sixties* songbook.
It's by some guy named Roy Orbison.
It's called "Only the Lonely."

Gimme a Beat

All week long, I listen to the twenty-two songs on Miss Person's CD.

They all sound alike.

You ever go in a store and hear a song and think you know it, but you can't think of the title because there are no voices singing and instead of guitars there are harps and trumpets and violins, and the rhythm is too slow or too fast, and really, this song that you think you know, that you think might be one of your favorite songs if you heard it the right way, sounds like Wheeler Diggs punched it in the stomach?

That's what all the songs on Miss Person's CD sound like. Like punched-in-the-stomach versions of themselves.

Not that I've heard half these songs before, anyway. Most of them are from before I was born. "Seasons in the Sun." "Smells Like Teen Spirit." "Who Put the Bomp (In the Bomp-Bomp-Bomp)." "The Theme from *Family Ties.*"

"So, what's it going to be?" asks Mabelline Person.

"'Forever in Blue Jeans,' by Neil Diamond," I say.

I like that name, Diamond. If I can't wear a diamond tiara at Carnegie Hall, I can at least play a Diamond song at the Perform-O-Rama.

"Fine. Let's get cracking." Miss Person flips a rhythm switch. "Ultimately, you'll be playing this with Rock Beat number three, but for now—"

Metronome.

What's Weird

Wheeler Diggs keeps following me home.

What's Really Weird

Wheeler Diggs and my dad are doing his latest Living Room University class together. Wheeler Diggs is making puff pastry. In my kitchen.

And on days when Mom calls and says she'll be home late, Wheeler stays and eats Mom's dinner. Which is most days.

And after dinner, he stays and does his homework.

I don't know what is weirder, Wheeler Diggs eating my mom's dinner or Wheeler Diggs actually doing his homework.

I think maybe it's the homework.

"Wheeler," says Dad. "It's nearly seven o'clock. Won't your dad be getting home soon?"

Wheeler shoves his stuff into his backpack.

"Do you want to bring him some éclairs?" Dad asks.

"Nuh-uh. Thanks anyway."

"Do you need a ride?" says Dad.

Ride? My dad is offering to drive?

"Nuh-uh. I just live over on Loon, remember?"

"Okay, then. We'll see you tomorrow?" says Dad.

"Dad," I say, "tomorrow is Wednesday. I've got my lesson." I've been practicing "Forever in Blue Jeans" for a week. I have to say I'm pretty good. Good enough, maybe, that Miss Person will declare me a prodigy after all.

"Do you mind hearing her lesson?" Dad asks Wheeler.

"I've heard her practice. It couldn't be any worse," he says.

Dad laughs. "See you tomorrow."

If at First You Don't Succeed

Miss Person puts her glass of ginger ale to her forehead, like she's trying to soothe a headache. "Wagner's Aunt Alice," she says. "Let's try it again, this time just the left hand."

I play the left-hand part. Without the melody to cover it up, I can hear rotten notes popping up all over the place. They are clunky and awful and as far from prodigy as you can get without giving up entirely.

"Hear that? Do that part again."

I do it again.

"Again."

I do it again.

"Again."

I do it again.

"Again."

I do it again.

"Once more."

I do it again.

"Better," she says. "Do it again."

I do it again.

Miss Person scribbles some notes on a yellow paper. "Okay," she says. "Here's the plan. All this week I want you to play the left hand only—just the left hand. The following week, we'll put both hands together again. Then we'll add the pedals the week after that." Miss Person counts on her fingers. "That will leave us one more week to get you perfect for the Perform-O-Rama."

She keeps on talking about practicing and how there's a long way to go before I'm performance ready and that I haven't even added the real percussion yet.

I don't say anything.

If I do, I know I'll cry.

The only person I ever let see me cry is my dad.

And he is in the kitchen puffing pastry with Wheeler Diggs.

And That's When I Decide

I'm going to quit.

Quitting

It is no big deal that I am quitting.

It isn't.

It really isn't.

It's not like quitting the piano.

That would be a tragedy.

People in movies only quit the piano when their wife dies or they get amnesia or they lose their arm in the war.

And even then, they don't quit forever, because one day they are sitting there thinking about the good old days when they still had a wife or a memory or an arm and they notice that there is a piano in the room and they walk over and they press a key, a single key, and then another and another and suddenly they're playing the piano again and they decide that life is worth living. And they are happy. And pretty soon they get a new wife and their memory comes back and they learn to play lots of songs written for one-handed piano players.

I would play the piano if I had only one hand.

If it was the right hand.

Not the left hand, though.

I can't play with my left hand.

I would have to practice all the time if I only had my left hand.

All the time.

Which, if I was a prodigy, I wouldn't have to do because I would be so talented that all I would do is read the music once and then I would sit down and play and it would be perfect. Even the left-handed parts. Perfect.

Which I can't.

Which is why I'm quitting.

Which is what I am going to tell my dad.

If Wheeler ever leaves.

Go Figure

Wheeler stays for dinner.

Then he stays to do his math homework. We're learning units of measurement. How many ounces go into two and a half cups? How many ounces go into three pints?

"Easy," says Wheeler.

He scribbles the answers in his notebook. Twenty ounces. Forty-eight ounces. He doesn't even look at the measurement chart.

"Bakers know these things," he says.

I don't know these things. I know how many mistakes I can make in a single bar of music (fourteen). I know how many times I want to play "Forever in Blue Jeans" again (zero). I know how much I want Wheeler Diggs to go home (infinity).

"Wheeler, it's seven o'clock," says Dad.

Wheeler shoves his notebook into his backpack. "Thanks for helping with science," he says.

"No problem," says Dad. "See you tomorrow."

"See ya," says Wheeler. "See ya, Zsa Zsa."

I stare at my measurement chart. "Sixteen ounces in a pint," I say. Wheeler turns and shuffles down the hall. The front door clatters shut. "Thirty-two ounces in a quart. Four quarts in a gallon. Nine gallons in a firkin."

Dad flips a dish towel onto his shoulder and sits down next to me. "What's a firkin?" he says.

"I thought bakers knew these things," I say.

"I'm still workin' on firkins," says Dad. He bumps my shoulder with his. I'm supposed to bump him back, but I don't.

The only sound in the room is the scrape of my pencil. *16 gallons*, I write. *23 quarts*. Finally, Dad pushes himself up from the table.

"How come Wheeler's own dad doesn't help him with his science homework?" I say.

Dad sits back down. "You know Wheeler's parents are divorced, right? Well, Wheeler lives with his dad and his dad works late."

"Why doesn't he help him when he gets home?" I say.

Dad runs his palm along the tabletop. "Have you ever met Wheeler's dad, honey?"

I shake my head.

"Me neither. I asked Wheeler to describe him once. Wheeler said he had a racing stripe—a long line of suntan down his left side from driving so much with the window open."

I laugh, picturing a grown-up Wheeler-looking person with a half-tanned face.

"Seems Wheeler's dad just isn't happy unless he's in motion. If he's not working, he's jogging or mowing the lawn or going out for long drives in his pickup. He's as uncomfortable caged up in his house as—"

"As you are outside of ours?" I ask.

Dad chuckles. "Guess John Diggs needs to feel the wind in his hair as much as I need to feel this linoleum under my feet."

"What about what Wheeler needs?" I ask.

Dad pats the table a couple of times. He looks at me like he does when he's helping with my homework. Patient. Waiting for me to figure things out for myself.

"Wheeler needs to be here?" I ask, but even as I do, I know the answer.

"And what about you?" asks Dad. "What do you need?"

All this time I've been waiting to tell my dad that I'm quitting, but now that he's ready to listen, I'm not ready to say it.

"I need to know how many gallons are in two and a half firkins," I say.

Dad pulls his chair tight up to mine. "Let's figure it out."

Still Quitting

Thursday, I don't play the organ.

Friday, I don't play the organ.

Saturday, I don't play the organ.

Saturday night, me and Mom and Dad are watching TV. During a commercial Dad asks, "How come you're not playing the organ?"

I just shrug my shoulders and then that show about the guy who's this crazy neat-freak detective comes on and Dad starts watching TV again.

But Mom is watching me.

I don't look at her, but I know she is watching me.

I should tell them I'm quitting.

I should.

But I don't.

I just watch the detective on TV get all weirded out about being in a crowded elevator. I watch and Dad watches and eventually Mom stops watching me and goes back to watching TV.

I will tell them I'm quitting tomorrow.

Who Knew?

Dad is out of eggs. Usually we have stuff delivered by GiddyUpGrocer! but it is Sunday and our GiddyUpGrocer! order won't come until Tuesday and Dad is in a popover crisis. You can't make popovers without eggs.

"I'll get some," says Mom. She gives Dad a wink, then turns to me. "You want to come with?"

Mom never asks me. It's faster just to go out by yourself and dash into the market without dragging somebody else along who might start begging for a bag of Better Made potato chips. Which I wouldn't do, because today is the day I am going to tell everybody that I am quitting, and thinking about telling everybody that I am quitting is making my stomach all twisty and I couldn't eat anything, anyway.

Soon as we're in the car, Mom flips on the radio. WCLS. There's this show on that I've never heard before, with all these teenagers playing classical music. There's a studio audience and every time one of the teenagers finishes playing, the audience hoots and claps and the host has to beg them to settle down so he can do his interview.

"So, Daniel, how long have you been playing the cello?" he asks and Daniel Cello-player says, "Since I was a kid," and this makes the audience laugh. Mom laughs, too.

"You stay in the car, okay?" says Mom. "I'll get the eggs and be right out." She turns off the car, but leaves the key in the ignition so the radio keeps playing.

Daniel Cello-player is talking about how he started playing the cello when he was five. "But I didn't get good at it until I was eight. Before that I didn't practice much."

"And how much do you practice now?" asks the host.

"It depends on how much homework I have," says Daniel, and the audience laughs again. I don't get what's so funny.

"Probably I practice about two or three hours a day," he says. "Plus I'm in orchestra at school, so that's another hour."

Four hours a day.

"And this piece that you played today, the Bach Cello Suite no. 3, how long have you been working on that?"

"That's a competition piece. I started working on it in the fall. I still mess it up sometimes." The audience laughs again. "This part still trips me up," he says, and then he plays for a minute or two. I don't hear any tripping.

The audience doesn't, either, and they hoot and clap some more.

Then the host asks Daniel if he has a girlfriend, which seems kind of nosy to me, but Daniel doesn't mind.

"I do. Her name is Kelly," he says.

"And does it bother Kelly that you spend so much time practicing when you could be going to the movies with her?"

Mom opens the car door and slides in, setting the bag of groceries at my feet, just as Daniel is saying that Kelly understands that when you love something as much as he loves the cello, you make sacrifices. Besides, Kelly plays the oboe and practices more than he does. This makes the audience laugh again, and then Daniel starts in on another number.

"Beautiful," says Mom. "He makes it sound so easy, doesn't he?"

He does. It sounds like the notes are lifting themselves off the cello strings. It's hard to believe that a teenager with homework and a girlfriend is making that sound. Who knew you'd have to work four hours a day to make something sound so easy?

"What do you say we drive around for a couple of minutes, so we can hear the rest?" Mom asks. "The popovers can wait."

I nod, and as we turn a corner, the grocery sack tips over and a bag of Better Made potato chips slides out.

"Crunch quietly," Mom says.

Key Change

I'm not quitting.

Instead, I will practice four hours a day. I will get up early and practice. I will come straight home from school and practice. I will stay up late and practice.

At the Perform-O-Rama, I will play and people will hoot and applaud and stomp their feet until the judges tell them to settle down.

And after I perform, radio people will show up to interview me and ask how much I practice and how I got to be so good in such a short time and if I have a boyfriend. And I will give them witty answers and they will ask me to play "Forever in Blue Jeans" one more time and I will.

And sometime, weeks later, my mom will be driving along listening to WCLS and they'll play my interview and she will drive right past work so she can keep listening to me.

What I Do

1. Get up.
2. Eat breakfast.
3. Go to school.
4. Do school stuff.
5. Come home from school.
6. Practice "Forever in Blue Jeans."
7. Eat dinner.
8. Do homework.
9. Practice "Forever in Blue Jeans."
10. Go to bed.
11. Repeat and repeat and repeat.

Dinner

Even though Mom is home, Wheeler is staying for spaghetti, so I set an extra place at the dinner table.

"Was that your Perform-A-Palooza piece you were playing when I came in?" Mom asks.

"Perform-O-Rama," I say. "Uh-huh."

"And when's the Perform-O-Rama?"

"In two weeks," I say. "The day after my birthday. You are still taking me, right?"

Mom nods, filling in the calendar she keeps in her head. I wonder if she's adding my birthday to the calendar, too, or if it was already there alongside her meetings and deadlines and presentations.

Then she looks at Wheeler. "And you're the kid who eats my dinner when I'm not here?"

Wheeler nods.

"I couldn't let him leave," says Dad. "He's co-creator of the Amazing Maple Tart, debuting tonight at Chez Us."

"Debuting?" Mom asks. "Half of it is already eaten."

"We gave some to Hugh," says Wheeler.

"And we had to test it," says Dad.

The Amazing Maple Tart is amazing. I catch Mom sneaking a taste.

"This is good," she says. "I may have to double your Living Room University budget if this is the return we get on our investment."

Dad grins.

"You know," says Wheeler, "we should sell this."

"There's only half left, Wheeler," says Dad. "And it's lopsided. Who's going to buy half of a tart?"

"I mean whole ones," says Wheeler. "We can bake them and sell them to restaurants and grocery stores." Wheeler waves a fork in the air. "Oh! And to the snack bar at Danny's Chomp and Bowl! Bowlers will pay big bucks for something that tastes like food. And we can get our own delivery van with our company name painted on the side—maybe Tarts 'R' Us or Kings of Tarts or something—and we'll be so famous that little kids will see our van and come running out of their houses like we're in the ice cream truck and we can sell them slices for a quarter and if they don't have a quarter we can sometimes just give them a slice because we'll be millionaires."

I've never seen Wheeler like this before, all sparkly-eyed and grinning.

"Listen to him!" Mom laughs. "All worked up about a crazy dream."

"What's so crazy about it?" I say, and then, of course, I know.

Wheeler's just a kid. He can't drive all over Eastside. He can't sell things to strangers. He can't talk tarts with restaurant owners and snack bar people.

And neither can my dad.

Lunch

The Fireside Scouts' month of cookie selling is up and there are empty seats in the lunchroom again, but when I go to sit in one, Wheeler Diggs calls me to his table.

"Sit here, Zsa Zsa," he says.

And I do. I sit there and then Colton and Henry and Danny start asking if I brought any cookies and I tell them no, but I've got a shoe box full of mini éclairs.

"What are those?" says Wheeler.

What are those? Wheeler is asking what are those? *He should know; he made them,* I think, and when I start to tell him so, I see this look in his eyes. This please-don't-tell-these-guys-I-wear-an-apron-at-your-house-every-afternoon look.

So instead I open the shoe box and let everybody find out about éclairs for themselves. Which they do.

"Thank you," says Colton. He says it all polite and with a little smile. And he's wearing a new shirt. And his hair is combed. Did I miss something? Is it picture day?

No, everybody else is wearing the same scraggedy clothes they always do.

"Yeah," says Henry. Then he swallows a big gulp of air so he can burp out a proper thank-you for me.

"And Earth's temperature rises five degrees," says Wheeler.

"Huh?" says Henry.

"Didn't you read your science book, slob?" asks Wheeler. We're studying global warming. Our science book says that cows burp methane gas and scientists think that's making a gas blanket around the world and heating everything up. Which is what Wheeler tells Henry.

"You're saying I burp like a cow?" says Henry.

"Yeah," says Wheeler.

"Cool."

"I thought it was cow farts," says Danny.

"Book says burps," says Wheeler.

"Termite farts are worse than cow farts or burps," I say. I learned it when my dad was taking Bugs to Bucks. There's this whole chapter of fascinating facts about bugs and why you should kill them. Termites chew on houses, but they don't digest them very well, so they're always farting up wood chip gas and releasing even more methane than cows do.

"Is that in the book?" asks Danny, who is suddenly interested in science.

"No," I say.

"Then how do you know?"

I don't want to tell them about Bugs to Bucks. Because then they'll ask if my dad kills bugs for a living and I'll say no and they'll say what does he do and I'll have to tell them that he stays in our house all day earning degrees that he'll never use.

"Because she's smart, fool," says Wheeler. "She hasn't damaged her brain sitting around inhaling her own fumes." Thank you, Wheeler.

And then Colton says, "Yeah."

And then the bell rings.

And then Colton picks up my empty shoe box and throws it in the recycling bin for me.

"See you in science," he says.

Smitten

Me and Wheeler walk in the house just as Hugh is finishing his coffee. "Think about it," Hugh tells my dad.

"Yes. Well," says Dad. "Yes. I'll think about it."

"Bye, Wheeler," says Hugh. "Bye, Zoe."

"Think about what?" Wheeler asks.

I open the fridge. Miss Person is due any minute. It is our last lesson before the Perform-O-Rama this weekend and I want everything to go perfectly.

The fridge is crammed with eggs and whipping cream and all the other stuff my dad needs for his Patty Cake, Patty Cake: Make Some Cash course.

"The case of Vernors is in the basement. I had to make room up here," says Dad. "Bottom of the toilet paper shelf."

I go get Miss Person's ginger ale while Wheeler and Dad talk about whatever it is that Dad has promised to think about.

"You should totally do it," says Wheeler when I come back upstairs.

The Vernors is warm. Miss Person will need extra

ice. Dad's started storing flour in the freezer, "like the pros do," so I have to move four bags of cake flour to find ice.

Dad changes the subject. "Anything interesting going on in school these days?"

"Your daughter has a boyfriend," says Wheeler.

I drop the ice. "What?"

"Colton Shell is smitten," says Wheeler.

"Smitten?" asks Dad.

"Smitten," says Wheeler.

"Well," says Dad. "Well."

"He's not smitten," I say. I don't exactly know what *smitten* means, but it sounds okay, like I wouldn't mind if Colton Shell was smitten. Like it might actually be kind of good to have somebody smittening me.

"He is," says Wheeler. "Wore a new shirt for her. Threw her garbage away at lunch."

"Garbage pickup is a clear indicator of smitten-hood," says Dad.

Smitten. Colton Shell. I have goose bumps.

"Close the freezer door, Miss Smitten," says Dad. So maybe I was cold.

I try it again. I say the words in my head: *Colton Shell is smitten with me.* More goose bumps. And my stomach is twisty. In a good way. And I hear this sweet ringing sound, like church bells or . . .

"Doorbell," says Wheeler.

Doorbell?

"Go open it, Goober," he says.

Oh yeah. Open it. Miss Person. What is she doing here?

Oh yeah. My lesson.

How My Lesson Goes

Perfect.
Right hand. Perfect.
Left hand. Perfect.
Pedals. Perfect.
Rock Beat #3. Perfect.
Perfect.
Perfect.
Perfect.
"Handel's cousin Hannah," says Mabelline Person.
On her way out the door, she hands me a Perform-O-Rama info sheet with the competition rules and stuff about registration and parking and directions and *See you there* scribbled across the bottom in purple ink.
"You did great, kiddo," says Miss Person. "Whatever happened to you today, make sure it happens again this weekend."
Colton Shell, I think.
Goose bumps again.

The Next Day

Emma Dent says that Lily Parker says that Sally Marvin heard somebody tell Danny Polzdorfer that Colton Shell likes me.

And she says that if I want, she'll tell Colton Shell that tomorrow is my birthday, which she remembers from when I used to be her best friend. And she says how come I'm not having a birthday party and if I am having a birthday party how come she isn't invited. And if I want to I can sit at her table at lunch.

And I ask her where Joella Tinstella is.

Joella Tinstella is out sick today, she says.

I tell her, "Thanks, but I've got a place to sit." *At Wheeler's table*, I think.

And she says, "At Colton's table."

And I say, "Yeah."

My *Boy*friend

All afternoon Wheeler Diggs is calling Colton Shell my boyfriend. Only he says it like this: *boy*friend.

At the drinking fountain he says, "Your *boy*friend wore another new shirt today."

After science he says, "For such a shrimp, your *boy*friend eats a lot of Tater Tots."

"Too bad your *boy*friend didn't study for his science test," he says on the bus.

"He's not my boyfriend," I say.

But I blush and Wheeler calls him my *boy*friend again, and then we sit there for a long time until the bus gets to my stop and I get off and Wheeler gets off and Wheeler says tell your dad I'll see him tomorrow and I just stand there watching Wheeler walking, past my house, past Warbler Drive, all the way down to Loon Lane. The corner house has a plastic stork stuck in the grass with an "It's a Boy!" balloon attached to its beak, and when Wheeler walks by, he punches the stork in the stomach.

Where's Wheeler?

Wheeler isn't on the bus this morning.

And he isn't in class.

Wheeler skipped school. On my birthday.

Maybe he's sick like Joella Tinstella.

Sick. On my birthday.

Right before lunch, Mrs. Trimble makes us partner up for this afternoon's Spelling Showdown and Emma asks if I will be her partner. The only other person without a partner is Colton Shell, which makes me all nervous and jumpy, and so I tell Emma okay but only if we can practice our spelling words at lunch and she says okay, which means that I have an excuse for not sitting at Colton's table. Which is good.

Dialogue

Me and Emma sit in the corner of the lunchroom to practice for the Spelling Showdown.

"Dialogue," I say.

"Dialogue?" asks Emma. "Can you use it in a sentence?"

"Our dialogue was interrupted by a handsome stranger before you had a chance to wish me a happy birthday," I say.

"Dialogue," says Emma. "Die-a-log."

"Dialogue," I repeat.

"D...I...A..."

"Hey." It is Colton Shell.

"Hey," says Emma. She's got her head cocked to one side so she can look up at Colton through her eyelashes. This is her "I'm so pretty" look. I remember her practicing it in the mirror back when we were best friends.

I wonder if I'm supposed to look at him through my eyelashes, too, but now it would probably look stupid, me and Emma tilting our heads exactly the same way. Like I'm copying her. Like I'm taking girl lessons or something. Which I could probably use.

"You doing spelling?" asks Colton.

"Yeah. We're doing spelling," says Emma.

Maybe I should try tilting my head in the other direction. I could still peek at him through my eyelashes, but I wouldn't look exactly like Emma. Not exactly.

"I hate spelling," says Colton.

"Yeah. I hate it, too," says Emma. "It's dumb."

"Yeah," says Colton. "It's dumb."

Maybe I should just tilt a little bit. Not as far over as Emma. Not like a puppy dog or anything. Just a little.

"Your neck okay?" Colton asks me.

I nod.

"Well, happy birthday," says Colton, and he hands me a yellow envelope. "It's a card."

"Thank you," I say.

"Okay," says Colton. And then he walks back to his table.

Emma Dent gasps, and grabs my hands. "He totally likes you so much. Did you see the way he blushed? And how he said happy birthday? He's soooooooooo cute. You are sooooooooo lucky. You know, Lily Parker likes Colton, too, but she just decided that she liked him yesterday and he already liked you except that she wasn't really sure that he did and she thought that maybe it was just a rumor because she was so sure that

Colton would like her over you any day, but he doesn't. He likes you. Aren't you going to open your card? I can't wait to see what it says!"

I can. I can wait a long time. At least until after lunch. At least until Emma Dent is not leaning over my shoulder memorizing every word so she can tell Lily Parker and everyone else. I tuck the card into my spelling book.

"We've got to practice," I remind her. "Dialogue."

"Yeah. Whatever," says Emma. "Dialogue."

The Kitchen Is Closed

I play "Forever in Blue Jeans" and
I play "Forever in Blue Jeans" and
I play "Forever in Blue Jeans."

And I keep playing because there is nothing else to do. Dad and Wheeler are in the kitchen and they say I can't go in there, not even for a Vernors, not even to pass through to get to the bathroom, not even to ask Wheeler why he wasn't in school today.

I can't go in the kitchen because Dad and Wheeler are finishing my birthday cake, which I know is really more of a wedding cake because Dad has to make one for Patty Cake, Patty Cake: Make Some Cash, so instead of a pudding-in-the-middle cake from a box like we usually have, I'm getting a three-tiered birthday cake with a gazebo on top.

Which is way better than a pudding cake from a box.

Or a grocery-store cake in the shape of a shoe.

The Words

The Perfectone *Hits of the Seventies* songbook has notes and instructions like *crescendo* (get louder) and *pianissimo* (play very softly), but it doesn't have the lyrics to the hits. It is pretty easy to figure out where Neil Diamond would sing the "forever in blue jeans" part, just by how the melody goes, but I don't know the rest of the words.

So when I play I sing,

> *"LA dee da*
> *da-DA-dee-DA-dee DA-da*
> *LA dee da*
> *LA da-DA-da-DA-da-da*
> *LA dee da*
> *da LA da dee da*
> *Forever in blue jeans."*

Like that.

"Your cake is almost ready," Dad calls from the kitchen. "Just a few more minutes."

I flip the Rock Beat #3 switch.

I count.
oneandtwoandthreeandfourand
Bum
  Bum
    Bum
      Bum go the pedals.

It's kind of sad that there are no words.
oneandtwoandthreeandfourand
Bum
  Bum
    Bum
    Bum
        "Birthday cake
        A cake-y cake that Dad and
        Wheeler make

        The finest birthday cake in
        His-to-ry
        For this prodigy
        Forever in blue jeans."
Bum
  Bum
    Bum
      Bum

"Mom will cry.
She'll hear me play and she will
Nearly die.

They all will beg and they will
Plead with me
To play Carnegie
Forever in blue jeans"

The phone rings just as I'm getting to the part that *Hits of the Seventies* calls *the bridge*. This is where Miss Person has me flip on the oboe and bassoon switches to make this part of the song sound serious.

I sing the bridge while Dad answers the phone.

"I'm gonna win
I'm gonna win a big fat shiny trophy or two.
My mom and dad will be glad.
They'll say 'Horowitz who?'"
Bum
*   Bum*
*   Bum*
*   Bum*

"Honey?" calls Dad. "You can come in now."

My cake is beautiful.

The bottom tier is covered with pink and orange and yellow roses. There are leaves around the sides, too, silvery green, and vines winding up the fat columns that hold up the other tiers.

"We didn't have real columns," says Wheeler. "So your dad frosted some toilet paper tubes."

The second tier has a pond. It is silvery and there's a little wooden bridge over it and trees and flowers and a bench where a tiny cake person might sit to fish or read a frosting newspaper.

But best of all is the third tier. Instead of a gazebo and a plastic bride and groom on top, there's a grand piano.

"I made it out of Mars pan," says Wheeler.

"Marzipan," says Dad.

"The keyboard is kind of lumpy, and one of the legs is too short," says Wheeler. "You can eat it if you want."

But when I tell him I don't want to, that I want to keep it, he smiles. Now I know why Wheeler didn't come to school. He was here all day. Making me a piano for my birthday.

"It's perfect," I tell him.

"It's crooked."

"It's a crooked kind of perfect," I say.

"So," says Dad. "Who wants the first piece of cake?"

"Shouldn't we wait for Mom before we cut it?" I ask.

"Well," says Dad. "Well. No. That was your mom on the phone. There's a work crisis. A ledger emergency. She's going to have to stay late and . . ."

"And?" I ask, but I know. Mom is going to have to work all weekend, too. Which means . . .

"Well," says Dad.

"She can't go to the Perform-O-Rama," I say.

"Well," says Dad. "Well. No."

What Dad Says

Who needs a Perform-O-Rama anyway?
Who needs it?
Really?
The competition?
The pressure?
Who needs judges telling you you're talented?
You know you're talented.
I know you're talented.
Wheeler knows you're talented.

I know what we'll do. We'll have our own Perform-O-Rama here! Right here. We'll dress up fancy and have candles and we'll put Vernors in champagne glasses. We could have hors d'oeuvres and I could print up programs. I learned how to print programs in Party Smarty.

You'd like that, wouldn't you?
Programs?
And Vernors?
Just the three of us?
Who needs anything more?

What I Say

I do.

And Then

I slam my chair into the table so hard that the tiers of my birthday cake wobble, which is what is going to happen if you don't have real columns and you balance the whole thing on stupid frosted toilet paper tubes because you're too much of a freak to get in the stupid car and drive to a baking supply place and get real columns like a regular person.

Which you wouldn't have to do anyway if you could just go to a real baking class at a real baking school, which is what normal people do because they aren't all weirded out by the idea that there might be real live human beings sitting next to them and a real teacher and maybe even a graduation ceremony where a real person might hand you a real rolled-up diploma instead of having you tear your suitable-for-framing diploma out of the back of a book.

And what good is a stupid framed diploma to anybody anyway if after you learn how to scuba or fly or plan parties or bake you never go out in the world and scuba or fly or party or bake for anybody, anyway?

And that's what I say. Then I say, "What good is

working hard and learning to play the stupid Perfectone D-60 if nobody ever hears me?"

And Dad says, "I hear you."

And I say, "That doesn't count."

Directions

I am hiding in my room, listening to one of Mom's Horowitz CDs. Loud.

Someone knocks on the door.

"Go away," I yell.

It's Wheeler. "I've got cake, Goober," he says.

I let him in.

"It's Zsa Zsa," I say.

Then we eat cake.

And when we finish, Wheeler goes out to the kitchen and gets us each another piece and we eat that, too.

Wheeler turns off my CD player. "He's gonna take you," he says.

"He'll try, but he won't be able to. He'll get nervous and we'll get lost and then we'll end up back here." My voice cracks and Wheeler thinks I'm choking on cake so he goes and gets us each a glass of milk.

Which we drink.

"I was mean," I say. "It's not his fault. He can't do this."

"He can do it," says Wheeler.

"He can't. It's like he physically can't. It's like . . ."

I try to think of something that Wheeler can't do so he'll understand. "It's like if you wanted to burp upside down. But you can't. Your body just won't let you. That's what it's like for him."

"He'll do it," says Wheeler.

We sit there for a while, pushing cake crumbs around our plates.

"You were pretty mad out there," Wheeler says.

"You were pretty mad yesterday," I say.

"Was not."

"You punched a bird."

"A fake bird," he says. He shoves his hands in his jacket pockets.

"I thought you might not come back here ever," I say.

"You should have known I wouldn't miss your birthday, Goober."

"I should have known you wouldn't miss cake." Wheeler laughs and for a second I feel like everything is okay, and then we hear Dad in the kitchen talking to himself.

"I-94 to Huron Avenue exit. Take a left. Seven miles north past the Birch Valley Mall. Right at Bixby. Left at Erie."

And then he says those words again.

And again.

And again.

They are the directions to the Perform-O-Rama.

Planning for the Worst

Wheeler stands up.

"Come on," he says, but I don't move.

"Come on," he says again and he grabs my hands and pulls me up and out of my bedroom and into the kitchen and onto a kitchen chair. He sits next to me.

Dad sits next to Wheeler. He has the Perform-O-Rama info sheet in his hands and keeps rolling it up in a tube and then flattening it out on the table and rolling it up and flattening it out again.

"Where's your cell?" Wheeler asks, and Dad gives him the cell phone.

"And your *Yellow Pages*?" Dad gets him the *Yellow Pages*.

Wheeler pushes up his jean jacket sleeves. "Okay," he says. "What's the worst that could happen?"

"We could get lost," Dad says.

Wheeler punches in the phone number for Marty's Eastside Wreck and Tow. "Marty's is now speed dial number one," he says.

"There could be bad weather," Dad says.

Wheeler looks up the number for the National Weather Service. "Speed dial number two."

"A crazy truck driver could try to run us off the road," says Dad.

"State Police, speed dial number three."

"We could run out of gas or get a flat or . . ."

"Got that covered with Marty," says Wheeler. "What else?"

"We could run late and the hotel could give away our reservations," says Dad.

"Birch Valley Hotel, number four."

"I could run out of cash."

"Michigan Independent Bank, number five."

"We . . . we could get really hungry?" says Dad.

This is ridiculous, I think. "Or monkeys could descend from the sky."

Wheeler pages through the phone book. "Bust-A-Burger, speed dial number six. Detroit Zoo, number seven," he says.

Dad laughs. "You think the zoo handles flying monkeys?"

"I'll add the Humane Society, just in case," says Wheeler. "That's number eight."

"Tsunami," I say.

"Arnold's Rent-A-Lifeguard, number nine."

"Alien invasion," says Dad.

"Squash-Um Pest Control, number ten."

"We could forget which speed dial is which," I say.

"Just remember number eleven. That's me. I'll remember the rest," says Wheeler.

Thump

Thump.

Thump.

Thump thump thump thump thump thump thump thump thump thump.

Dad is hauling a giant wheelie suitcase up from the basement. I remind him that he only has to pack for one night.

Thump.

"You never know what you're going to need," says Dad.

I roll my eyes but Dad doesn't see because he is already halfway down the hall, his suitcase wheels clicking over the linoleum.

"I have to go," says Wheeler.

I nod.

"He's going to do it," says Wheeler.

I nod again.

"So what's the matter with you?"

"My mom can't go," I say.

"Big deal," says Wheeler.

"It *is* a big deal!" I say. "She was supposed to go. She was supposed to hear me play!"

"She's heard you play," says Wheeler. "A couple of times, at least."

"She missed my birthday," I say. "My eleventh birthday! How many birthdays has your mom missed?"

"All but the first one," he says.

And even though he smiles his lopsided smile and tells me, "Good luck, Goober" and "Remember number eleven," I feel like Wheeler Diggs has punched me in the stomach.

My Card

It is dark.

I am in bed.

It is dark and I am in bed trying not to think about Wheeler's motherless birthdays.

I can hear Dad in his room repeating the directions to the Perform-O-Rama while he packs his suitcase. "I-94 . . . Birch Valley Mall . . . Erie . . ."

And then I hear the rumble of the garage door and Mom's Saturn chugging into the garage and the garage door closing again.

Clink. Mom's keys on hook.

Creeeeeeeaaaaak. Closet door open.

Scrape. Coat hanger.

Another creak. Closet door closed.

Mom's heels thud on the linoleum. *Thud thud thud.* She is walking into the kitchen.

She is looking at my cake, I bet.

Now she is going to come to my room and wish me a happy birthday and try to make up with me by giving me some lame present. Which I will not accept.

Here she is, thudding down the hallway.

Past my door.

Down the hall to her own room, where I hear her tell my dad that he can finish packing in the morning and she has had a hard day and can't they just turn off the lights already?

And then everything is quiet.

No "Happy birthday, honey."

No lame present.

Not even a card.

A card. Wait. I got a card today.

I flip on the lights and look for my spelling book—there it is. Colton Shell's yellow envelope.

I remember how he gave it to me. "It's a card," he said.

It was kind of nice how he said that. Thoughtful. Like he didn't want me to think that maybe it was something else. Something unimportant, like, well, I don't know. But anyway, he wanted me to know it was a card. Which is sweet.

And probably he also said it because Emma Dent was right there and he wanted to send me the signal not to open it in front of her. He wanted me to know it was a card and it was special and he had written something personal in it for my eyes only and he thought that if I didn't know it was a card, I might open up the envelope right there just to find out what was inside and then that nosy, buggy little gossip Emma Dent would have seen his deep private thoughts about his feelings for me.

The envelope is sealed, so I shove my finger in the little space at the top and that tears the envelope a bit, but I know Colton doesn't mind. He understands things like this. Colton Shell understands.

On the front of the card is a fat hippopotamus. The hippo is holding a piece of birthday cake in one hand and a giant fork in the other. It is wearing clogs.

This is what the card says:

> *Hip-hippo-ray for you today!*
> *Let's cheer and cheer again!*
> *We'll have a hippo-lot-o'-fun*
> *Because today you're ten!*

Except Colton has scribbled out the word *ten* and written in the number eleven and added a bunch more exclamation points. Like this: 11!!!!!!!!!!!

And then he signed it. *Colton.*

Not *Love, Colton.*

Or *Happy birthday, Colton.*

Or *Best wishes, Colton.*

Just *Colton.* And a couple more exclamation points.

I hate exclamation points.

Four Dreams and a Phone Call

Dream #1

I am at the Perform-O-Rama.

I am playing "Forever in Blue Jeans."

I am wearing a tiara and I am playing "Forever in Blue Jeans" and I am perfect.

Dream #2

I am at the Perform-O-Rama.

I am playing "Forever in Blue Jeans."

I am wearing a tiara and I am playing "Forever in Blue Jeans" and my tiara slips down over my eyes and I can't see my music and I make a huge mistake.

I make a huge mistake and everybody hears it.

And then Colton Shell pops out of the Perfectone D-60 and starts singing.

Bum

   Bum

      Bum

         Bum

"Hippo-ray

You'll have a happy happy hippo-day

You'll cheer and cheer and cheer and cheer again

Because you're ten
Forever in blue jeans."

Dream #3

I am at the Perform-O-Rama.

I am playing "Forever in Blue Jeans."

I am wearing a tiara and playing "Forever in Blue Jeans" but the judges can't hear me play because Colton Shell is singing and Emma Dent is sitting on a couch and telling the judges how nobody wears tiaras anymore and how cute Colton Shell is and how lucky I am that he likes me because really Colton Shell could like Lily Parker, who wouldn't be caught dead in a tiara.

The judges are nodding.

One of the judges is my mom.

Dream #4

My mom is judging the Perform-O-Rama.

I am wearing a tiara and playing "Forever in Blue Jeans."

I am perfect.

I think I'm perfect.

I'm not perfect.

My mom shows me her judging sheet. It is filled with red marks—one for each wrong note.

And then a phone rings and everybody turns and looks and there in the audience Vladimir Horowitz is pulling a cell phone out of his tuxedo pocket.

"Hello?" he says. He looks at me.

"It's for you."

Vladimir Horowitz Makes Mistakes

One of the ways you can tell that Vladimir Horowitz was the best ever piano player was that when he screwed up, nobody cared. They loved him anyway.

One time, my mom played me a CD of Vladimir Horowitz screwing up. He had retired twelve years earlier and then changed his mind and said he wanted to play concerts after all and he was going to do this big comeback concert at Carnegie Hall. People went crazy. Rock-star crazy. They camped out on the street to get tickets—fancy grown-up Carnegie Hall people stood in the cold all night because they wanted to see Horowitz play.

Which is a lot of pressure to put on a guy.

And on the day of the concert, Horowitz showed up six minutes before he was supposed to go onstage and that made everyone nervous and he was nervous and when he finally did get onstage the audience cheered and then he sat down and it was totally quiet.

Nobody said a word.

They didn't even breathe.

They waited.

They waited.

Then he started playing.

And then he made a mistake. Actually, he made a couple of mistakes.

"There," said my mom, "and there."

I wouldn't have even known they were mistakes if my mom hadn't told me. But she did. And then she said those mistakes didn't matter because it was Horowitz. And Horowitz was not about perfection. He was about joy and art and music and life. And those things have mistakes in them.

"I make mistakes, too," I said.

"And when you are as good as Horowitz," said my mom, "yours won't matter, either."

The Birch Valley Hotel
and Conference Center

We're in the lobby of the Birch Valley Hotel and Conference Center and my dad can't move.

He was moving fine a minute ago. He was cha-cha-ing through the parking lot singing about how he didn't get us lost once and Wheeler should have put the *Birch Valley Sentinel* on his speed dial because this is front-page news.

Then we walked into the lobby.

Then Dad froze.

The lobby of the Birch Valley Hotel and Conference Center has cathedral ceilings and marble-looking floors and every sound you make in it echoes.

Phones ringing.

Elevator bells pinging.

Wheelie carts thumping.

There are kids pulling suitcases and kids riding suitcases and kids unzipping suitcases and trying to shove other kids inside them. There are kids with balloons and kids yelling that they want balloons and kids getting yelled at for popping other kids' balloons.

And there are teenagers standing around in circles

and whispering and squealing and then looking around and whispering again.

There are parents, too. Parents in the registration line. Parents in the restroom line. Parents pulling kids out of suitcases.

People walk fast around us and between us, saying every year it is the same thing and can't anybody figure out a better system for getting these packets distributed and there's no way that Lindsey girl is only nine years old and Peter has moved on to his own private instructor now and where's the john and I swear if you pull on that ficus tree again you will not go swimming in the hotel pool tonight, do you hear me, mister?

And there are lights, too. Rows and rows of bulbs in the ceiling and chandeliers at the registration desk. There are yellow Christmas lights in all the ficus trees and lit-up signs for RESTROOM and ELEVATOR and EXIT.

Worst of all, there are two enormous blue searchlights sweeping the room. Every few seconds they flash in Dad's face.

And Dad can't move.

"Dad, you okay?" I ask.

He says nothing. He is watching the searchlights as

they reach their destination: a red carpeted platform and the biggest organ I've ever seen.

"The M-80," says a man in a suit.

"Huh?" says Dad.

"Impressive, isn't it? Top of the Perfectone line. A real firecracker!"

"Dad," I say. "Dad, we have to go register."

Dad looks at the man. He has a button pinned to his suit. ASK ME ABOUT AN UPGRADE!! it says.

Dad obeys the button. "What's an upgrade?" he asks. The man smiles. "Follow me."

Dad follows.

I follow Dad.

The Upgrade man takes us past the spotlight to the Perfectone M-80 platform, which is surrounded by red velvet ropes.

"I'm really not supposed to do this," he says, looking around. "The Perfectone M-80 is too powerful an instrument for a little space like this lobby. If we're not careful we could shatter all the lightbulbs in the place—and then where would we be?"

"In the dark," I say.

"Heh-heh, you're a pip, kid," he says. Then he turns his back to me and asks Dad what model organ I have now.

140

Dad looks over his shoulder. "What do you have now?"

"A headache," I say.

"You're a pip all right, kid. Go get a balloon."

"Dad, we need to register," I say again.

I follow Dad's eyes to the registration table—or where the registration banner is, anyway. You can't see the table because there are so many people around it. Parents and kids and balloons and more guys in suits with Upgrade buttons on their chests.

There is no one else here on the M-80 platform. Just me and Dad and Mr. Upgrade. It's almost peaceful here, like we're on our own little Perfectone island, surrounded by a sea of sharks. Noisy sharks. With luggage.

Dad is not leaving the island.

Miss Person to the Rescue

"Back off, Merv."

It's Miss Person.

"Mabelline," says Mr. Upgrade. "I was just telling the gentleman here about the exciting features of the Perfectone M-80."

"Tchaikovsky's checkbook, Merv. He just bought a D-60 in December. Find another fish."

Miss Person pulls us to the shore of M-80 Island. "You'll have to watch out for guys like Merv," she says. "This place is crawling with them."

She pulls a thick manila envelope out of her purse. My name is written on it in fat purple letters. "I got your registration packet for you."

Dad nods. He looks pale. "I'd like to sit down," he says. "Someplace quiet."

Miss Person hands Dad his room key. Then she pulls her marker from her purse.

"Hand," she says.

Dad looks puzzled.

"Give me your hand." She writes *6:30—Meeting Room G* across Dad's palm.

"That's where Zoe will be playing, six-thirty P.M.,"
says Miss Person. "You can meet her there."

Dad nods. "Okay," he says.

"Now go to your room," she says.

Dad looks at me. "You'll be okay?"

"She'll be fine," says Miss Person.

"I'll be there to watch you play, honey," Dad tells me.

"I'll be fine," I say. I try to mean it.

And then Miss Person pulls me off the platform.
"Come on. There's someone I want you to meet." She
grabs my arm and we cut through the waves of kids
and parents and suitcases and ficus trees to an elevator
packed full of Upgrade men. She squishes us in.

"Sixth floor," says Miss Person.

I look back into the lobby.

My dad is still standing there on M-80 Island.

He waves at me. And even though I know the mark
on his hand is just Miss Person's note, from here it
looks like a giant purple bruise.

Mona

"This is Mona," says Miss Person.

Mona is eleven, like me. She is also pretty and blond and has pale pink nail polish on and she looks a little like Lily Parker.

Which is not like me.

"Mona has been my student for six years," says Miss Person. "This is her fifth Perform-O-Rama."

"This is your first?" Mona asks me.

"Uh-huh."

"The first can be scary," she says, "but Mom and I are pros. We'll get you through it."

Mona's mom is Judy. Judy is blond like Mona and has perfect teeth. Judy looks like Lily Parker will look when she grows up. Except that Judy smiles.

"You can go, Mabelline," says Judy. "We'll take it from here."

Go? Miss Person is going?

She has ripped me from my dad and now she's dumping me here in a sixth-floor hotel room with toothy blond strangers?

"You girls will do great today," says Miss Person.

"I'd come hear you if I wasn't judging the adult rounds."

She's not going to be there? Wait a minute, I want to say. What if I get lost? What if I get stage fright? What if I lose my music?

"What if I make a mistake?" I say.

Miss Person laughs. "Just keep playing."

How It Works

Judy pulls the information sheets out of my Perform-O-Rama competition packet and spreads them across the hotel bed.

"Do you know how this works?" she asks me.

I don't know.

Judy picks up a pink sheet. On the top in bold letters it says, HOW IT WORKS. "You'll play twice. Once tonight and once on Sunday," she says. "Each time, you'll play for two judges who'll be reading your music and noting any mistakes. They'll also make general comments about tempo and style and selection. They award points for good things and take away points for mistakes."

"Your lowest score is dropped," says Mona.

"That's right," says Judy. "So you won't have to worry about one judge having a prejudice against your style or selection. Only the three best scores are added up."

"The top five kids in each age group get trophies," says Mona.

Judy pulls out the competition schedule.

"There are ten eleven-year-olds playing this year," she says.

"Is Mika here?" asks Mona.

"He is," says Judy.

"He's cute," says Mona.

"He plays well, too," says Judy.

"Yeah," says Mona. "And he's cute."

"Margaret Barstock is back again, too."

"Oh, she's really good. Last year she took second," says Mona.

Judy keeps reading the names of the eleven-year-olds and Mona keeps saying stuff about who is good and who is nice and who one time forgot his music in his hotel room and had to run up three flights of stairs to get it and barely made it back by the time his name was called and had to play while he was panting like a dog and he still won a trophy.

Now I am nervous.

I wasn't before, but now I am.

I never thought about other kids playing.

I thought about me and "Forever in Blue Jeans" and winning and getting invited to play at Carnegie Hall and Mom in the audience cheering and thinking that maybe I could be the next Horowitz.

But there are other kids here.

Kids who have done this before.

Kids with trophies.

"There's an hour before you girls have to play. Do you want something to eat?" asks Judy.

Eat? Is she kidding? Maybe trophy kids can eat, but just the word *eat* makes my stomach twist. In a bad way.

"No, thank you," I tell Judy.

"I packed plenty of sandwiches. Mona? You want salami?"

"Salami?" says Mona. "Are you kidding? I'll hurl!" She reaches for two cans of pop: one for herself and one for me. "Can you imagine that? Getting up to play and launching salami?"

My stomach twists again. I try very hard not to imagine launching anything. "That doesn't happen, right? Nobody has ever thrown up at a competition before?"

"I never saw anybody puke," says Mona. "But one year a kid fainted. He was playing 'Green Acres' and then he started tilting to the side and then *whoosh!* Slid right to the floor. It was awesome."

Awesome?

"He hadn't had anything to eat all day," says Judy. She edges a zippy bag of sandwiches toward us.

Mona edges it back. "So his mom went rushing to help him, but before she got there he was back up on the bench again playing 'Green Acres' like nothing ever happened. Awesome."

"Did he get a trophy?" I ask.

"No, but he got a standing ovation," says Mona. "Moral of the story?"

"Eat something," says Judy.

"Just keep playing," Mona says.

What It Is Like at Carnegie Hall

There are balconies at Carnegie Hall.

People who sit in balconies wear shiny ball gowns and have their hair twisted up fancy on their heads and carry purses that are just big enough for a pair of tiny binoculars that they use during the concert to get a closer look at your brilliant fingering. The men wear tuxedos.

When the balcony people first get to Carnegie Hall, they can't see the stage. All they see is a huge velvet curtain with golden fringe and tassels.

The lights dim.

The curtain rises.

And there is a glossy black grand piano.

Nobody says a word.

They don't even breathe.

They wait.

They wait.

And then a spotlight hits the stage and you walk out and everybody cheers and you glide gracefully to the piano and stand in front of it while the crowd goes wild and you smile a gracious smile and curtsy and raise your dainty hand to wave and the crowd gets even louder and you curtsy once again.

This is called making an entrance.

What It Is Like
at a Perform-O-Rama

You don't make an entrance at a Perform-O-Rama.

Because when you finally find Meeting Room G, where you are supposed to play, there are already a bunch of people there who are left over from the Children Age Ten competition and there is no stage and no velvet curtain so even if you wanted to make an entrance, you couldn't.

And there are no balconies.

Everybody sits in cold metal folding chairs in Meeting Room G, and except for the judges and the kids in the competition, everybody is wearing jeans.

And you don't read the program because there is no program. Instead, everybody keeps poking around in their conference packets and pulling out HOW IT WORKS or THINGS TO SEE IN BIRCH VALLEY or the MEET THE PERFECTONES! brochure.

There are three organs up at the front of Meeting Room G. In the center is the Perfectone M-80, which MEET THE PERFECTONES! says has

- *three (3!) keyboards*
- *twenty-four (24!) pedals*

- *one hundred and six (106!) orchestralike sounds*
- *thirty-nine (39!) toe-tapping rhythms.*
- *Plus!! a real cherry bench and warm cherry veneer, which make it an elegant addition to any home decor!*

To the right of the M-80 is the J-70, which has two keyboards like the D-60, but more pedals (!) and orchestralike sounds (!) and rhythms (!). It also has a cherry veneer and bench and looks lovely in any setting!

On the far left sits the two-keyboarded, ten-pedaled, realistic-looking walnut-veneered, vinyl-benched Perfectone D-60.

MEET THE PERFECTONES! does not call the D-60 elegant.

It does not say the D-60 is lovely.

MEET THE PERFECTONES! says the D-60 is a cozy choice.

Cozy.

Like a pair of socks.

Round One

Judy and Mona sit near the front, where they can hear the music best.

I sit in the back by the Meeting Room G doors so that when my dad comes in he will see me right away and won't get all freaked out by how many people there are.

In addition to my competition packet, I have three photocopies of "Forever in Blue Jeans" in my lap. One for me. One for each judge. I follow the notes with my finger. I try to make up words to go with the melody.

Bum

   Bum

      Bum

      Bum

"Please don't puke . . ."

What rhymes with puke? Fluke? Kook?

Where's Dad?

It's almost time for the competition to start.

"Mika Soddenfelter?"

It *is* time for the competition to start.

A cute boy stands up. His mom straightens his tie. He hands the judges their copies of his music.

x

154

"Mika will be playing 'Theme from *Kojak*' on the Perfectone J-70. Whenever you're ready, Mika."

Mika smiles. He is cute. Even when he sits down on the cherry bench at the Perfectone J-70 and his back is toward you, you can tell he is cute.

"Theme from *Kojak*" sounds cool. Way cooler than "Forever in Blue Jeans." I watch Mona bobbing her blond head in time with the music. Way cooler. When Mika finishes, he is not smiling so much, but Mona and Judy and the judges and a lot of the people up front are. They are clapping, too.

Back here by the Meeting Room G doors, not so many people are clapping.

Back here, they are talking about mistakes and tempo and just because something is jazzy doesn't make it good and how come you can't bring food in here?

The Meeting Room G doors open.

A bunch of people hurry in. A bunch of other people hurry out.

There's some kind of spring on the doors that makes them pull shut. *Swoosh-BANG!*

"We'll remind people that they may only enter and exit the room between performances," says a judge. "And if our volunteer will please make sure the doors close gently?"

Everyone turns and stares at the white-haired lady in a Perform-O-Rama Mama T-shirt. "Sorry," she says.

"Next up, Victoria Dewsbury."

Victoria Dewsbury walks to the front of the room.

Dad must be in the hallway. He's probably too nervous to come in.

"Victoria will be playing 'Gettin' Jiggy Wit It' on the Perfectone J-70."

Victoria plays.

There is clapping. Victoria's parents cheer. The back-of-the-room people mutter.

"I'd hardly call that jiggy," says one.

A snooty-looking lady lowers her glasses. "It's a good thing the Perfectone people rewrite this music for the student songbooks. That girl never could have handled the original composition. Imagine if she'd attempted one of the classical pieces."

Classical pieces? Why didn't Miss Person tell me there were classical pieces?

The doors open. People rush in. Other people rush out.

I peek into the hallway. No Dad.

Swoosh! No bang. Instead, a quiet *click*. The Perform-O-Rama Mama smiles.

"Andy Markowitz."

Andy Markowitz plays "Big Girls Don't Cry." His mother cries.

Now none of the back-of-the-room people are listening. They are flipping through their packets. They are reading MEET THE PERFECTONES! Their kids are playing hangman. One guy is sleeping.

The doors open. *Swoosh-click.* The doors close.

Still no Dad.

"Olivia DiMaggio."

Olivia is the first one to use the Perfectone M-80. She plays "The Theme from *The Young and the Restless.*"

The sleeping guy snorts.

The front of the room claps for Olivia.

The back of the room doesn't.

"Young and the Restless? More like the Old and the Comatose," one guy mutters.

"Shut up, Harry," says a lady sitting next to him. "How would you like it if people said things about Becky's playing?"

Thing is, I don't understand what Harry is talking about. All the kids who played sounded good to me.

Margaret Barstock plays Mendelssohn's "Spring Song" on the Perfectone M-80. It's a classical piece. A pretty one. And I don't hear any mistakes when she plays, except you can tell by her face when she turns around that she must have made some, because Margaret Barstock has tears in her eyes and her face is all red.

Harry starts to say something about spring coming late this year, but Mrs. Harry shoves a Tic Tac in his mouth.

Just keep playing, I think.

Four more kids until my turn.

Three.

Two.

"Becky Depschak?"

Harry's daughter stands.

"Becky will be playing 'Istanbul (Not Constantinople)' on the Perfectone J-70."

Nobody is playing the D-60. Nobody.

And everybody has a parent here. Everybody.

Where's Dad?

Becky starts playing. Then Becky stops playing. I hear Harry whisper, "It's okay, baby. You can do it."

There's no way Becky can hear him way up there, but Harry whispers anyway, and then Becky starts playing again. And when she's done, Harry claps and everybody else claps and Becky shuffles back to her dad with her head down and Harry hugs her and calls her champ and says how about we go get a Bust-A-Burger? And Becky nods and the Depschak family leaves.

A few other people leave, too.

But nobody comes in.

Swoosh-click.

My Turn

It's my turn.

Dad's not here and Miss Person's not here and Mom's not here, but it is my turn.

People have shifted all the chairs around in Meeting Room G and there's not much of an aisle left, so I have to weave around people to get to the front of the room where the judges are. And when I get there I hand them my music, but I still have my competition packet in my hands. All the other kids handed their packets to their parents before they played. I didn't have anybody to hand my packet to.

"Which instrument will you be playing?" asks a judge.

"The organ," I say.

"Yes, of course," she says. "But which one?"

"Oh," I say. "The Perfectone D-60."

And then the judge tells everybody that I will be playing "Forever in Blue Jeans" on the Perfectone D-60. Somebody snorts. I hope it is the sleeping guy in the back.

Where am I supposed to put my packet?

I put my music on the music stand, but the packet is too fat to go behind it. I could sit on it. No. The floor. I drop my packet on the floor. Somebody laughs.

Okay.

I look at the music.

Okay.

Here goes.

I flip the Rock Beat #3 switch and get ready to count *oneandtwoandthree* . . .

I can't hear Rock Beat #3.

I push the volume pedal all the way up.

Nothing.

I flip the rhythm switch again.

I flip it again.

Flip flip flip.

Nothing.

Now there is a judge by my side.

"Looks like nobody has used the D-60 today." She laughs. She pushes the On button and the Perfectone D-60 wheezes to life, with Rock Beat #3 booming so loud some little kid starts crying and has to leave.

Swoosh-click.

I turn off Rock Beat #3.

I fix the volume.

I take a deep breath.
I turn on Rock Beat #3.
oneandtwoandthreeandfourand . . .
Bum
  Bum
    BumBumBum
My foot slips on the pedals.
Just keep playing.

Just Keep Playing

I say it four more times—once for each mistake.

Just keep playing.

Just keep playing.

Just keep playing.

Just keep playing.

And then "Forever in Blue Jeans" ends.

I slide to the edge of the Perfectone D-60's vinyl bench and put my foot on the floor except I don't step on the floor, I step on my packet, which goes shooting out from under me and I almost fall, but I don't.

Just keep walking, I tell myself.

I keep walking.

One of the judges picks up my packet and hands it to me.

And then I hear people clapping and I see Judy waving me over and I go to where Judy and Mona are and I sit down next to them and Judy gives me a hug.

"Nice job," she says.

"I made mistakes," I say.

"Everybody made mistakes today," says Judy.

"You kept playing," says Mona.

"Mona Kinzler?" calls a judge. Mona hands Judy her competition packet.

"Have fun, honey," says Judy. She gives Mona a hug.

"Mona will be playing Bach's Toccata and Fugue in D minor on the Perfectone M-80," says the judge.

Vladimir Horowitz Says

Perfection itself is imperfection.

That's what Horowitz said.

I heard it on that show that I watched with my mom. The voice-over guy said that Horowitz meant that it wasn't enough to get all the notes right. When you play the piano, you have to get the heart right. Which is harder than getting the notes right.

Each note can only be right in one way. A B-flat is a B-flat is a B-flat. A robot can get a B-flat right.

But getting the heart right is something only a person can do. And the ways to do it are as many and as different as there are people in the world.

Hearing Mona play, I know that she has found one of them.

When Mona Plays

Everyone is smiling.

Judy is smiling and the judges are smiling and Mika is smiling and I am smiling and I bet if Harry Depschak and his family weren't at Bust-A-Burger, they'd be smiling, too.

Because when Mona plays you feel like smiling.

And singing.

No. That's not right.

It's not that you feel like singing actual words. Not lyrics.

It's that even though you know that Mona is reading the music and her fingers are pressing the keys and her feet are tapping the pedals and the sound is coming out of the Ultra-Gold fashion weave speakers of the Perfectone M-80, you feel like the music is coming out of you.

Like it does when you are singing.

Dad

Mona and Judy walk me to Room 415 at the Birch Valley Hotel and Conference Center.

We knock.

"Dad?" I call.

"Coming!" says Dad.

He opens the door just wide enough to stick his head out.

"Everything okay?" Judy asks.

"Fine," says Dad. He doesn't look at Judy. "Well. Well. Thank you for taking care of . . ."

"No problem. She's a delight," says Judy.

"See you tomorrow," Mona tells me.

"Uh-huh," I say.

"Eleven o'clock. Meeting Room G." Mona looks at Dad when she says it.

"Okay," I say. "See you tomorrow."

And when they get all the way down the hall and turn the corner and can't possibly see us anymore, Dad opens the door.

The hotel room looks like our house. Our kitchen tablecloth is spread across the table by the window and Dad's blue checkered sheets are on his bed. There is a set of red checkered sheets on the other one. There's a picture of Mom and me on the nightstand next to Dad's alarm clock. In the bathroom are our yellow towels and in the soap dish is a half-used bar of Zest that Dad must have brought from home, too.

"I was trying to get things comfortable," says Dad. "You never know how well these people clean." Dad's cleaning supplies are under the bathroom sink. "It's a good thing I did, too. You do not want to know what was hiding between the mattresses."

He's right. I don't.

"Well," says Dad. "Well, it was dirty. And I got dirty cleaning it. And it was late and I wasn't thinking and ... well ..." Dad sits on the edge of the bed. "I washed my hands."

He holds up his hand. Where Miss Person had written *6:30—Meeting Room G* there is now a fat purple smudge.

"I'm sorry, honey," he says.

"It's okay, Dad," I say. "You can come tomorrow."

"Flying monkeys couldn't keep me away," he says. "You want to eat?"

"I'm starving," I say.

And then Dad drags his Living Room University backpack out of the closet. Inside are sandwiches on

Rolling in Dough bread, Bake Your Way to the Bank cookies, two cans of Vernors, and a bag of Better Made potato chips.

And we sit at the little hotel table with our tablecloth on it and Dad turns on the TV and we eat.

"Just like home," says Dad.

It's for You

Dad's in the shower when his cell phone rings.

Mom, I think. *Calling to ask how I did.*

And I don't want to tell her.

I don't want to tell her about the organ not being turned on and my foot slipping on the pedals and making all those mistakes.

"Can you get that?" hollers Dad from the shower. "It's probably your mom."

I get it.

"Hello," I say.

"Hey, Goober."

It's Wheeler. Hooray for Wheeler!

"Zsa Zsa," I say.

"Listen, Zsa Zsa," he says.

I listen. I hear a weird squeaky sound.

"Did you hear that?" he says.

"What was it?"

"I burped. Upside down. I've been practicing."

I laugh. I can't help it. I laugh and I keep laughing.

"You called me so you could stand on your head and burp?" I say.

"I'm not standing on my head. I'm hanging off the side of my bed."

"Then you're not really upside down," I say.

"I'm almost upside down." He squeaks again. "How about that?"

"Very impressive." I mean it. Not everyone would put in that kind of effort.

"How'd it go?" he asks.

And I tell him.

I tell him about Dad doing such a good job getting us here and about the noisy lobby and the Upgrade man and Dad not making it to the performance room and how I goofed up so much. And how I just kept playing.

"Cool," he says.

And then I tell him what was really cool. I tell him about Mona and how when she plays you feel like your whole body is filled up with music—like singing.

And he says, "You play like that."

"What?" I say.

"You play like that. At school, when you played 'Green Acres.' And when you think nobody is paying attention. You play like that."

"I do?"

"That's why me and your dad are always singing in the kitchen."

They sing in the kitchen?

"You can't hear us because you're singing, too," he says.

"You can hear me singing?"

"Of course we can hear you, Goober," he says. "Someday we're all going to have to learn the words."

I laugh again.

Wheeler laughs, too.

And Wheeler's laugh sounds like singing.

Round Two

The next morning, I'm sitting in the back of Meeting Room G again, but this time Dad is with me.

"How does this work?" he asks.

I pull the HOW IT WORKS sheet out of my competition packet. He reads it.

"So, if you do better today, one of yesterday's scores will be dropped?"

I'd told Dad about yesterday. After Wheeler called and Dad was out of the shower, I told him how I made all those mistakes.

"But you kept on playing?" Dad said. His eyes got wide when he said it. I could tell he was proud.

"Everybody does," I said. "You can't just get up and walk away every time you mess up. You'd never get anywhere."

I'd told him about Mona, too. How she played.

And I made sure we got here extra early today, so he wouldn't miss her.

Dad looks for Mona's name on the schedule. "So, she plays first?"

"Yep," I say. We go in the reverse order of yesterday, so Mona's first and I'm second.

"We're just about ready to start," says a judge. "Would our volunteer please let the people in the hallway know?"

The white-haired volunteer is gone. Today's volunteer is a big guy in a red plaid shirt with a Perform-O-Rama Mama T-shirt stretched over it.

"We're starting, people," calls the volunteer. "Allegro, kids. Speed it up."

People flood into Meeting Room G. Becky Depschak and her family. Mika and his parents. Andy Markowitz and his mom.

Swoosh-click. The doors close.

Dad's leg starts bouncing. He rolls HOW IT WORKS into a tube and taps it on the back of the chair in front of us.

"You okay?" I ask him.

Dad uncurls the paper.

"I'm fine," he says.

"Mona Kinzler?" calls a judge.

Mona stands and hands her packet to her mom. She gives her music to the judges. She sits down at the Perfectone M-80. Everyone is quiet.

Mona plays.

Just like yesterday, everyone is smiling.

Dad is smiling.

His leg is not bouncing and he is smiling and he puts his arm around me and I feel like Mona's music is in both of us. Like it is in all of us.

When Mona finishes playing, everybody claps and Dad says, "Bravo."

Then the doors open and a bunch of people walk out and another bunch of people walk in and the smiles fade and people start talking again about how stuffy it is in this room and how come they don't let you bring food in here?

"You're next, huh?" Dad says.

"I'm next."

I look at my music. I hear it in my head. I hear myself singing and Wheeler singing and Dad singing.

But Dad is not singing. Dad is leg-bouncing. Tapping and bouncing and looking over his shoulder at the doors.

"I'm proud of you. It must be really hard to play in front of all these people," he says, looking at the doors again.

"You want to go?" I ask him.

"No," he says. He kisses me on the forehead. "I want to stay."

They call my name.

Swoosh-click.

I hand Dad my competition packet.

"You can go if you need to," I say. "I'll be okay."

"I'll just keep sitting," Dad says. "You go have fun."

I bring my music to the judges. "I'll be playing the D-60," I tell them.

I check the On switch.

The Perfectone D-60 is ready and wheezing.

And just as I am about to start, I hear it.

Swoosh-BANG!

The doors.

Poor Dad, I think.

Just keep playing, I think.

Rock Beat #3.

oneandtwoandthreeandfourand

Bum

   Bum

      Bum

         Bum

I play.

And even though I know that I am reading the music and my fingers are pressing the keys and my foot is tapping the pedals and the sound is coming from the Ultra-Gold speakers of the Perfectone D-60—even though I know all that—it feels like the music is coming from right inside of me.

And When I'm Done

I gather my music from the stand and slide off the bench and turn around and see that people are smiling. The judges are smiling and Mona and Judy are smiling and Becky and Mika and a lot of other people in the room are smiling.

And way in the back, by the doors of Meeting Room G, my dad is standing there smiling.

And next to him is my mom.

And she is smiling, too.

After

Dad is still clapping when I get to the back of the room.

"Thank you very much," I say. I curtsy. I don't think I have ever curtsied before. It feels good, though, so I do it again.

Dad looks a little pale. But he is still smiling.

"I'm going back to the room," he says. He gives me a big sweaty hug. "I'm proud of you," he whispers.

"Becky Depschak?" says the judge.

"Let's find a seat," says Mom.

Swoosh-click.

Becky Depschak walks to the front of the room as me and Mom find a seat behind the judges.

"Now how does this work?" asks Mom, and I hand her the HOW IT WORKS sheet.

"Becky will be playing 'Istanbul (Not Constantinople)' on the Perfectone J-70," says a judge.

Before Becky can flip the Merengue switch, Mom takes out a pen and marks up HOW IT WORKS, underlining "lowest score will be dropped" and "style and appropriate selection" and "top five performers earn trophies." Mom sees me watching her. She moves her pen down to the last line of HOW IT WORKS and circles two words.

"Have fun!"

Mom

Mom has a mirror in her purse.

Actually, it is two mirrors with a little hinge between them so you can open it and see if your makeup is the same on both sides of your face.

Or, if you angle it just right, you can use it to look over the Perform-O-Rama judges' shoulders and see what marks they are making on people's music sheets. Which is what my mom is doing.

She watches how many mistakes each person gets and reads the comments the judges write.

She has written down the names of all the competitors and drawn columns next to them, with little slash marks for each mistake. She writes down the judges' comments, too, in code, with plus signs and minus signs and stars.

This is how Mom has fun.

More Fun

Mika Soddenfelter finishes "Theme from *Kojak*" and Mom snaps her mirror shut.

"I liked that last one." She marks a two in Mika's mistake column, but adds a little star. "He should get extra points for having fun," she says.

Mika did sound like he was having fun.

In fact, everybody sounded like they were having fun. A lot more fun than yesterday.

"I'm sorry you missed Mona," I tell Mom.

"Missed me what?" I turn to find Mona and Judy standing behind us. I hope they didn't see Mom's mirror trick.

"Missed hearing you play," I tell her. "You were great again."

"Thanks," she says. "You were great, too."

"Awards aren't until four o'clock," Judy says. "Mona and I are going to the Birch Valley Mall for lunch. You two want to join us?"

When Mom looks at me, I nod and she pulls out her cell phone. "Let me check with Domestic Affairs," she says.

And then she goes into the hallway to call my dad, and Mona starts talking about how cute Mika is and how there is this boy at her school named Tony and how he looks like Mika except he's taller and has glasses and brown hair and green eyes and how he likes her and she likes him except he's not really her boyfriend or anything.

"Do you have a boyfriend?' she asks me.

And the first thing that pops into my head is Wheeler. But Wheeler is not my boyfriend. Wheeler is a boy. And he is my friend. And I think he's cute in a messy kind of way. But he's not my boyfriend. I think all that. And then I think how weird it is that I thought of Wheeler and not Colton Shell, who isn't my boyfriend either, but at least Colton Shell likes me. I mean, *likes me* likes me.

"No," I say.

And then Mom comes back in.

"Let's go," she says.

Money Talks

By the time we get to Bust-A-Burger, we are starving. It took us forever to find the Bust-A-Burger because the stores in the Birch Valley Mall are the same as in our mall at home except they are all rearranged, so even though you think you're near Bust-A-Burger because you can see Mango Tango and Twisted Mister Pretzel, really the Bust-A-Burger is on the whole other side of the mall but the Mango Tango people aren't sure whether it is downstairs next to Lo Fat's Kitchen or upstairs by Three Blond Mice. It is by Three Blond Mice.

There's a girl in the booth across from us who is wearing her Fireside Scout uniform, but instead of her badge-sash thing she has pulled a Brat T-shirt over her scout blouse.

"I hate that Brat stuff," says Mona. Actually, she says "I hape fat Braff fuff" because her mouth is full of Bust-A-Burger, but I know right away what she means.

"Everybody wears it at my school," I say.

"Why would you wear something that says you are spoiled and mean?" says Mona.

"Maybe it's true," I say.

"Wouldn't that be funny if everybody wore shirts with true stuff on them?" Mona laughs. "Like 'No Mind of My Own' or 'I Hope This Shirt Makes Me Look Cool'."

"Aw, I remember wanting so badly to look cool," says Judy. She points her burger at my mom. "Do you remember Giggles?"

"Giggles!" says Mom. "Of course I remember Giggles!"

"What are Giggles?" asks Mona.

"They were just the absolute coolest jeans ever," says Judy. "They had a little polka-dot pattern on the pocket. And if you didn't have a pair you were just nobody."

"I hated that," says Mom. "I felt like such a loser."

Judy nods.

Mom used to worry about being a loser?

"They were so expensive. I saved up babysitting money for months to get a pair," says Mom.

"I wore mine until they fell apart," says Judy.

Mom takes another big bite of her burger.

"And now," says Judy. "I must pee."

Mona stands. "I'll go with you."

"Anyone else?" Judy asks.

Me and Mom shake our heads. We have really strong bladders. It is one thing we have in common.

When Judy and Mona are in the bathroom, I ask Mom if she wore her Giggles until they fell apart.

"I never ended up buying a pair," she says. "Your granddad worked at Ford then and there were layoffs." Mom takes a sip of her pop. "There were more important things to spend that money on. I had other jeans."

I think about this. About Mom wanting to be cool and having to spend her cool-jeans money on something else.

Then Mom says, "If you want one of those Snot shirts, we can get you one."

"Brat," I say.

"Pardon me?"

"Not Snot shirts, Mom. Brat."

Mom laughs at herself, which is kind of strange. I don't remember her ever doing that before, but she laughs at her mistake and says, "Right. Brat. If you want a Brat shirt, we can get you one."

I tell her thank you but I don't want one. And I really don't. But it feels good to be asked.

Mom says okay. And then me and Mom sit side by side and chew and watch our reflection in the

Bust-A-Burger condiment island until Judy and Mona come back.

And when they do, Judy is singing.

"Mom," sighs Mona.

"Blame Zoe," says Judy.

Mona blames me. "You played so well this morning, she can't get your song out of her head."

Judy knows the words?

She does.

> "Money talks
> But it don't sing and dance
> And it don't walk
>
> As long as I can have you here with me
> I'd much rather be
> Forever in blue jeans."

The Brat Scout stares.

"Mom!" sighs Mona again.

My mom looks at her watch. "We'd better get going."

We walk fast from the Bust-A-Burger side of the Birch Valley Mall to the Mango Tango side and then out into the parking lot where, even though I am eleven years old, my mom holds my hand all the way to the car.

The Formula for Success

$$(A\text{-}B\text{-}C) + (X\text{-}Y\text{-}Z) + \frac{((A\text{-}B\text{-}C)+(X\text{-}Y\text{-}Z))}{2} = Total\ Score$$

This is what Mom has written on the back of my conference packet.

"It's really very simple," she is saying. "The A, B, and C are the positive comments minus the number of mistakes minus the number of negative comments given by judge one. X, Y, and Z represent the same categories for judge two."

I don't understand, but I nod.

If Dad were here, he'd explain it to me. But Dad is not here. Mom said he had something he wanted to take care of at home, so he drove home early.

"Don't worry," she told me. "He has his cell."

I worry anyway.

"Now," she says, "since you are unable to tell me if anyone played better or worse on Saturday than they did today—"

"Except for me," I say. "I played worse."

"Except for you," says Mom. "Since you have no idea about anyone else, we will take the average of the totals for judge one and two to represent judge three." She points to the line with the number two on it.

I nod again. "Average," I say.

"Now all we have to do is plug the numbers from the grid into our formula and we'll have a pretty clear indication of what the final rankings will be," says Mom.

"Except for me and Mona," I say.

Mom doesn't say anything. She is plugging.

The Birch Valley Hotel and Conference Center ballroom is packed. So packed that Mom and Mona and Judy and me couldn't even find four seats together so Mona and Judy went up front to sit on the floor and me and Mom moved a ficus so we could sit on a windowsill.

Every seat is filled. Everywhere I look there are moms and dads and kids. There are Perfectone people with Upgrade buttons handing out MEET THE PERFECTONES! brochures and Perfectone volunteers in Perform-O-Rama Mama shirts shooing kids away from the trophy tables. People are saying no matter what, I'm proud of you and stop touching your sister and elegant cherry veneer and I am never eating another Bust-A-Burger as long as I live.

Up in the front of the room I can see Mona and Judy. They wave. I wave back.

Mom has her head down. She is still plugging numbers into her formula. She is smiling.

Mom looks pretty when she smiles.

"If you could all find your seats, please?" There is a Perfectone man at the podium in the front of the room.

"There you go," says Mom. She is done plugging. "Given the information we have—which is not complete, of course—the trophy list should look like this."

Mom hands me the conference packet.

Mika Soddenfelter
Roger Patel
Margaret Barstock
Andy Markowitz
Victoria Dewsbury

"Those are your winners," says Mom. She taps on the packet with her pen. "One, two, three, four, five."

"I'm Benjamin Bemmerman, regional manager for the Perfectone Corporation," says the man at the podium. The Upgrade button people clap.

"You need to put Mona on this list," I whisper to Mom.

"Congratulations to all of you who participated in this, the twenty-sixth annual Southwestern Michigan

Regional Perfectone Perform-O-Rama," says Benjamin Bemmerman.

"How did she play?" Mom asks me.

"Like Horowitz," I say.

Mom writes Mona's name at the top of her list. She scratches out Victoria Dewsbury. "Sorry, Vicky, no trophy for you," she says.

Poor Vicky.

"And how did you play?" Mom asks me.

I know I made mistakes on Saturday. Five of them. Maybe six. But this morning?

"I don't know," I say.

"How do you *think* you played?" says Mom.

"How do *you* think I played?" I ask her.

Benjamin Bemmerman starts announcing the six-year-old winners.

Why doesn't Mom answer?

Mona said I played great. Judy, too.

Why doesn't Mom say I played great?

"I suppose if your Saturday performance was really bad, my formula wouldn't work, anyway," she says. She is not smiling anymore. I think she is disappointed in her formula. Either that, or she is disappointed in me.

The Little People

Benjamin Bemmerman takes forever to announce the names of the trophy winners.

There are a lot.

"In the seven-year-old competition, fifth place goes to Danielle Bennet."

Some of the little kids scream when they hear their names and then jump up and down and their parents hug them and it takes them a really long time to even start walking to the podium to get their trophy. One kid cries.

"And our nine-year-old champion, Sylvia Karkatowski."

If I was going to get a trophy, I wouldn't cry.

Not that I'm going to get a trophy.

But if I was, if I was Mona or something, I wouldn't cry.

People don't cry at Carnegie Hall. They just nod and bow. Sometimes, I bet, they make speeches.

If I was Mona, I'd make a speech.

When you make a speech, you're supposed to thank the little people. Like that six-year-old who cried.

Then you thank your teachers and your friends and everyone who made this moment possible. Like Lester Rennet and Miss Person and Wheeler for calling on the cell phone and Dad for driving here.

"In third place, Minette Popper."

And I'd thank Mom for coming, even though there was a ledger crisis, for coming and hearing me play and taking me to lunch and telling me about Giggles and holding my hand in the parking lot even though she doesn't need to anymore.

And I would thank Vladimir Horowitz, too.

"Eleven-year-old competition . . ."

"In fifth place, Andy Markowitz."

Mom puts a check next to Andy Markowitz's name on her sheet. Her formula is working.

"In fourth place, Zoe Elias."

Mom does not check Zoe Elias off her list.

Zoe Elias is not on Mom's list.

Zoe Elias is me!

Mom jumps up and I jump up and Mom says, "Go get your trophy, Zoe!" and I go.

I am very professional.

I do not cry.

I take my trophy.

I bow. People laugh. Maybe I should have curtsied.

I do not make a speech. Instead, I walk back to Mom and watch her scratch out Margaret Barstock and in big fat letters write my name, ZOE ELIAS, in the fourth-place spot.

"Thank you, Mom," I say.

My Trophy

My trophy is shiny.

The bottom is marble—real marble—with two gold columns holding up another slab of marble with a gold plate that says:

FOURTH PLACE
ELEVEN-YEAR-OLD DIVISION

and then there's a sparkly blue column with the words PERFECTONE PERFORM-O-RAMA on it and then another slab of marble with a big gold musical note stuck on top. It is beautiful.

So beautiful, I don't take my eyes off of it until the award ceremony is over. And when I do look up, Miss Person is there, beaming.

"Beethoven's barbershop," she says. "Your first trophy. Congratulations, kiddo."

"Thank you," I say. My first trophy.

"In a couple of weeks, you'll get another gold plate in the mail," Miss Person tells me. "Your name will be engraved on it. You can stick it on your trophy with mounting tape."

My trophy.

This is my trophy. Those are my fingerprints smudged all over it. And in a few weeks it will have my name on it.

My name.

Zoe Elias.

I see Mona and Judy across the room. Mona waves her first-place trophy at me. I wave my fourth-place trophy back at her.

"Honey," says Mom. She is looking at her watch. "I'm sorry to hurry us out of here, but we've got to get going."

Cell-A-Bration

"I think you'd better notify Domestic Affairs," says Mom. She is driving with one hand and waving her cell phone around with the other. "Tell your dad we should be home in about fifty minutes."

I dial home.

"Hello?" says Dad. He sounds different. His voice is deep and formal, like he is about to make a speech.

"Dad?" I say.

"Zoe!" His normal voice is back. "How'd it go?"

I tell him I got fourth place.

"Whooooooo-hoooooo!" hollers Dad.

I hear a voice in the background. "What whoo-hoo?"

"She got fourth place," Dad says.

"Whooooooo-hooooooo!" It is Wheeler.

"So," says Dad. "You got a trophy. Isn't that better than having a piano?"

Is it?

I like having a trophy. Especially a shiny trophy that in a couple of weeks will have my name on it. But is it better than having a piano? Than playing piano music?

"I don't know," I say.

I liked playing today. I liked it more than I have ever liked playing before. I liked the way the pedals sounded and I liked the way the keys felt under my fingers and I liked the way Rock Beat #3 thumped around in my chest.

But the Perfectone D-60 is no piano.

"Let me have the phone," says Mom.

I hand it to her.

"Hello?" she says. "Yes. I know she got fourth place." Mom laughs. "Is everything going okay?"

Dad says something and Mom laughs again. "That's great. I can't wait to hear— Oh shoot," she says, "I've got another call. We'll be home in forty-five minutes. Okay. No. I'll call you back if I can."

Mom pulls the phone away from her ear. She presses a couple of buttons with her thumb.

"Hello? Sharon? Hey. How are things going with the ledger?"

It is Mom's office.

"No," she says. "No. I'll do it. I'll be in early tomorrow."

I rest my head against the car window.

"Terrific," says Mom.

She sounds happy.

Work makes Mom happy.

"Really, terrific," she says. "Sharon, you should have been there. People were actually tapping their toes. I was so proud."

Mom is not talking about work.

She is talking about me.

And she is happy.

On the Way Home

Mom goes back to talking about ledgers and deadlines and critical inaccuracies and fiscal years.

We drive by grocery stores and clothing stores and hardware stores and office supply stores. Bust-A-Burger. Coffee shop. Gas station. Bust-A-Burger. A subdivision full of houses that look exactly like the ones in East Eastside. A billboard for Bust-A-Burger.

When we go under an overpass, the window gets dark and I can see my reflection.

Grocery store. Bookstore. Party store. Tanning salon.

Me.

Gas station. Coffee shop. Subdivision.

Me.

Somewhere between my reflection and another subdivision, I fall asleep.

I dream I am playing the piano.

Taps

Tap tap tap.

I'm still in Mom's car but it's in our garage and Wheeler is tapping on my window. "Wake up, Goober."

"My name is Zoe," I say. I get out of the car.

"Let me see your trophy, Zsa Zsa."

"Zoe," I say.

"Elias," he says.

Elias.

Okay. Elias. I hand him my trophy.

"Cool," Wheeler says. He looks right at me and smiles his lopsided smile. My stomach gets twisty. In a good way.

"Is she awake?" calls Dad from the house.

"Are you awake?" Wheeler asks me.

I kind of feel like I'm not. This whole day has been too good. I kind of feel like I might be dreaming.

"Bring her in here. We have celebrating to do," says Dad.

Wheeler brings me in.

Mom and Dad are holding champagne glasses filled with Vernors. Dad hands another one to Wheeler and Mom gives one to me.

"To Zoe," says Mom, "who worked hard and played well."

"To Zoe!" says Dad. He taps his glass against mine.

"To Elias!" says Wheeler. His glass taps mine, too.

Mom and Dad and Wheeler take big gulps out of their glasses. I don't. I couldn't even if I wanted to. My throat has a lump in it.

"Are you going to cry, Elias?" says Wheeler.

I shake my head.

Everybody is looking at me.

It feels weird.

They need to stop looking at me.

How can I get them to stop looking at me?

"I have a toast," I say. "To Wheeler, who worked hard and can burp upside down."

Mom and Dad laugh. "To Wheeler!"

We all clink our glasses.

Then Wheeler raises his glass. "To Mr. Elias," he says, "who—"

"Hold up a second," says Dad.

"Let's have cake," says Mom.

Cake? We haven't eaten dinner yet.

"This is a cake-first kind of night," says Dad. "Wheeler, would you bring it out?"

Wheeler's grin gets extra goofy. He brings out the cake.

It's the top tier of my birthday cake. The one with the piano on it. Except now there are candles on it, too. And something else.

"It's you," says Dad.

It *is* me. A little marzipan me. Standing by the piano. Holding a trophy.

"Wheeler made it," says Dad.

The lump in my throat is back. And the twist in my stomach. Wheeler made it.

"Thank you," I say.

Wheeler nods. He doesn't say anything. I think Wheeler may have a lumpy throat, too.

"I'm sorry I missed your real birthday, Zoe," says Mom. "Dad tells me you didn't even make a birthday wish."

It's true. I didn't.

"Why don't you make one now?" says Mom.

I close my eyes.

I blow out the candles.

I open my eyes.

I am face to face with a smiling marzipan me.

Wishes

"I hope you wished big," says Mom.

I did.

"Did you wish for a piano?" she asks.

A piano? I didn't think to wish for a piano.

"We have a Perfectone D-60," I say.

"But you'd rather have a piano, right?" says Dad.

Yes. I would. But saying so would hurt Dad's feelings, I think.

"It's okay," says Dad.

I nod. Yes. Even if I never get another trophy, even if I never perform at Carnegie Hall, even if I am not the next Horowitz, I would rather play the piano. In my dreams, I play the piano.

"Good thing," says Mom. "Because you're getting one."

I'm getting a piano? I'M GETTING A PIANO? I could scream! I am screaming!

Mom and Dad are laughing and Wheeler is laughing and I am screaming, "I'm getting a piano!"

But how can I be getting a piano?

I ask this. "How can I be getting a piano? Aren't we still paying for the Perfectone D-60?"

"Your dad has been very busy since he left Birch Valley," says Mom.

"Rewind Used Music has a piano in stock that they would be happy to trade," says Dad.

Emma Dent's white baby grand?

"It's not fancy. An old upright. But it is in good condition and stays in tune."

A piano. I'm going to play the piano.

"Of course, we still have to keep making payments," says Dad.

"Can I do my toast now?" says Wheeler.

"Now seems right," says Mom.

"To Mr. Elias," says Wheeler, "who worked hard and got himself a job."

A job? Dad got a job?

Dad can't have a job.

A job means a boss. And other people.

Dad can't do people.

"You look worried, Zoe," says Dad.

"What kind of job, Dad?"

"Just the best job ever," says Wheeler. "Your dad is going to be a baker."

"You're going to sell Amazing Maple Tarts?" I ask.

"Well," says Dad. "Well, not unless Nunzio wants me to."

"Nunzio's Buns Nunzio?"

"Yeah!" says Wheeler. He is so excited he is hopping up and down. "Nunzio's Buns is on Hugh's UPS route and Hugh gave Nunzio a bunch of your dad's cookies and éclairs and breads and some of his Amazing Maple Tart—"

"*Our* Amazing Maple Tart," says Dad.

"And Nunzio told Hugh to tell your dad that he had an opening for an early-shift baker."

"I didn't think I could do it," says Dad. "You know . . ."

"You didn't think you could drive to the Perform-O-Rama, either," says Wheeler.

"But you did," I add.

"I did," says Dad.

"And you can do this," says Wheeler.

Turns out an early-shift baker works from two A.M. to six A.M., which is perfect for Dad because there is no traffic at two in the morning. Nunzio's Buns doesn't open to customers until six-thirty and once Nunzio is done training Dad there won't even be any other bakers there. Just Dad.

"You'll be great," I say. I raise my glass. "To Dad!"

Mom says, "To Leo!" and Wheeler says, "To Mr. Elias!" and then we all clink our glasses together.

Mom, I think. *We need to toast Mom, too.*

"To Mom!" I say. Who what? Who worked hard, and what? Wait. I know.

"To Mom," I say again. "Who stopped working hard long enough to hear me play."

"Thank you," says Mom.

"To all of us. And to being together," says Dad.

We are all happy to toast that.

Especially me. Especially that last part.

It was my birthday wish.

How It Is Supposed to Be

Me and Wheeler have our shoes off. Summer is almost here and it's warm. Wheeler's toes are freaky long.

"It's the one thing me and my dad have in common," he says.

We're sitting on my front porch in our bare feet and watching the sky turn pink and purple and waiting for the Rewind Music delivery guys who called to say that they were running an hour and a half late because they had to drop off a new turntable in East Eastside and the lady made them hook everything up for her, which was not in the work order, but they did it anyway and then her daughter said it was in the wrong spot and they needed to move it and so they unhooked everything and rehooked everything and by the time they were done they both had headaches and so they had to stop at Bust-A-Burger for dinner. But they are on their way now.

"Wheeler?" I say. I'm looking at his toes, the toes that are just like his dad's. "Wheeler? Where's your mom?"

"That is a long story," says Wheeler.

Just then the Rewind Music truck turns onto Grouse Avenue.

Wheeler stands and waves. The Rewind Music guys pull into our driveway.

"Are you Elias?" they ask Wheeler.

"She is," he says.

"Want to show us where this is going?" they say.

I do. But I also want to know about Wheeler's mom. And I want Wheeler to know that I want to know.

"I like long stories," I say.

"We've got all summer, Elias," he says.

We do. We have all summer.

I show the Rewind guys our living room.

"This thing goes back with us, right?" The thing is the Perfectone D-60.

"Yes," I say.

"And the piano goes in the same spot?"

"Yes."

I go back out on the porch to sit with Wheeler. The sun has dipped behind the garage roof and the porch is shady and suddenly cool. The Rewind guys set up a ramp on our porch steps. They roll the Perfectone D-60 on dollies—out of the house, down the ramp, into the truck. *Good-bye*, I think. *Thank you*. And before I can think about how weird it is that I just said thank you to a wheeze-bag organ, my piano is rolled out of the truck and set in the driveway.

My piano.

I have goose bumps.

"You cold?" asks Wheeler.

"I'm okay," I say.

Wheeler takes off his jean jacket. I've never seen him without his jacket on. He looks skinnier than I thought he would.

"Put this on," he says.

I put it on, but it doesn't stop the goose bumps. Putting on Wheeler's jacket gives me more.

The Rewind guys roll my piano up the ramp and into the house and into its spot in the living room.

"Are your parents here?" they ask me.

Mom is on the phone with her office. "What's the final tally?" I hear her say. "Does it all reconcile?"

"My mom is busy," I say. "And my dad is taking a nap." Dad had his first early-morning baking shift today.

"You can sign this then." They hand me a proof of delivery slip. I sign it. The piano is mine.

"The tuner will be by tomorrow afternoon," they tell me.

I nod. "Thank you."

The Rewind guys leave, clanging their dolly down the porch steps. It is so loud it wakes Dad. Even Mom gets off the phone.

"Your piano," says Mom.

Dad stretches and yawns. "I'm sorry it isn't a shiny new one."

It isn't shiny. Or new. It has a few scratches along the sides and the music stand is a little crooked. But it is mine.

"Try it out," says Wheeler.

Try it out?

"It's probably out of tune. I should wait until tomorrow. It will be perfect tomorrow," I say, but even as I say it, I'm sitting down on the piano bench and lifting the cover off the keys.

Dad waits.

Mom waits.

Wheeler waits.

They don't say anything.

They don't even breathe.

I rest my fingers on the keys.

I don't care if my piano isn't perfect yet.

I just want to play.

And I do.

> *"As long as I can have you here with me*
> *I'd much rather be*
> *Forever in blue jeans."*

Acknowledgments

. Nearly everything I know about writing I learned by working at an independent bookstore. The education I received while at Vroman's Bookstore was Ivy League, thanks to my professors: customers, colleagues, writers, artists, and friends. I am especially grateful to Sherri Gallentine, Jodi Kinzler, and the Northshire Bookstore's Stan Hynds, who read early bits of this story and only laughed when they were supposed to.

Lisa Wheeler read this story in its first incarnation—as a picture book. She told me it was funny, but it wasn't a picture book. It was a novel. I had no idea.

Susan Sandmore and Kelly Fineman read it as a novel, and their insight made it a better one.

Jeannette Larson had faith in this book when it was barely a scribble. Thank you, Jeannette, for your humor, grace, and dedication. You are the Horowitz of editors. I feel awfully lucky to have landed at such a welcoming and supportive place as Harcourt, and I'm grateful to Allyn Johnston and Jessica Dzundza for sharing their enthusiasm for this project.

My mother, Joanne Urban, told me to write what I had to and not to worry what she or anyone else would think. That may have been the bravest thing she's ever done. Thanks, Mom.

Marita Frey, Joe and Sharon Knipes, and the good folks at the Family Center of Washington County cared for my kids and gave me time to write.

My kids, Jack and Claire, inspire me to play, to see things fresh, and to make up words when regular ones don't fit. I'm still working on making up a word powerful enough to thank my husband and best friend, Julio Thompson, who pretends I am perfect, despite my dents and lopsidedness.

Finally, I must thank Marla Frazee and Myra Wolfe, my courage and counsel, without whom I would not be a writer.

A grant from the Society of Children's Book Writers and Illustrators helped make this novel possible.

LINDA URBAN grew up in Michigan with dreams of fame. Ballerina. Television star. Musician. She played the violin for a year, then begged her parents for a piano. Instead, her dad bought an organ at the mall. Although she has never competed in a Perform-O-Rama, she can still play the right-hand parts of "Up, Up and Away."

A former bookseller in California, Ms. Urban now lives in Vermont with her family. *A Crooked Kind of Perfect* is her first novel.

www.lindaurbanbooks.com